CW00406344

COTTON CANDY

BY

L. M. KIMBLIN

Copyright

Front cover artwork by Christine Southworth

Book cover design by Tara Collette

Book formatting by Sylva Fae

Printed by Amazon KDP

First printing edition March 2021

Acknowledgements

The world is a better place thanks to people who smile and provide encouragement when you need it most. My heartfelt appreciation goes out to the following people who have helped to make 'Cotton Candy' a reality:

First and foremost, my husband, Keith, who, despite whatever it was he was doing, would take the time to listen, advise and make endless cups of tea to keep me going. He makes a fine 'brew' accompanied always with a biscuit or three!

My much valued beta readers, Jan Riley (aka, Sylva Fae, author) and Maureen Jones, for their edits, suggestions and guidance. Not only acting as beta reader, Jan has also provided her expertise as developmental editor in the publication of 'Cotton Candy'.

Christine Southworth, member of the Neo Artists and member of the Society of Women Artists, for designing the cover and turning my vision of the protagonist into a striking piece of art.

Nick Davies, British investigative journalist, writer and documentary maker, for allowing me to reference his name and book, 'Dark Heart' and wishing me every success on my writing journey.

Past pupils, Simon Stones and Tara Collette. Simon Stones for his technical support (and patience) and Tara Collette for her Photoshop input and making sure the book cover was the best it could be.

For anyone who has lived through pain
and overcome the darkness.

*****

"For not an orphan in the wide world can be so
deserted as the child who is an outcast from a living
parent's love."

'Dombey and Son', Charles Dickens

PROLOGUE

'No child is born evil', cliché, I know, but it is something I have always held onto, in my mental portfolio, as I take on each new case.

A child is pushed, thrust into life, like all of us, with explosive, exuberant, vibrant excitement then immediately dependent, on those at hand, for survival first, for development later. Too many children, however, become victims, sad complex victims of circumstance, victims of background and I am the one left to try and understand and get to the root of what drives them, or what has driven them to such behaviours that society is shocked and sickened by.

I love my job. I love the feeling that I am doing a job that means something, that tests my strength, my stamina each day and brings with it so many challenges. A job where, thus far, I have gained a reputation as being one of the best in the field of Criminal Psychology. As such, I have been called upon to prepare a full report in a case where the behaviour of the offender has been called into question. My job is to explain the psychological and social factors that have contributed to the crimes that have been committed.

My job is to listen to the human story behind the 'monstrous' act, to assess, to understand, remain detached and, most importantly, non-judgemental. Not always easy.

I look up at the imposing brick red building in front of me, its stone steps leading to the heavy wooden door. I know that this institution holds within its walls young people deemed a threat to society, damaged and dangerous. The Victorian facade has history and I wonder who might have once lived here, back in the day? Some wealthy man of business or industrialist no doubt.

Surrounded by silver birch and lush green lawns, this grand and peaceful exterior disguises the turmoil of young minds that now reside within its walls. The juxtaposition of quiet and disquiet is immediately evident as I know what this building represents. Altham Grange, a secure home where young offenders are kept under lock and key for the protection of the public and, in most cases, for the protection of themselves.

Angie Ross. Aged 15. Sadistic, brutal, evil, wicked. The press had been the first to brand this teenager with all the usual condemnations and who could blame them? Despite the whys and wherefores nothing, absolutely nothing, will dispel the horror of her crimes in the eyes of society. From now on her actions will be a talking point, sensationalised, exaggerated, as people do in such conversations and as they remember.

Angie Ross. Complex? No doubt. Influenced? I am yet to find out.

PART ONE

CHAPTER 1

'Every man has his secret which the world knows not...'

Henry Wadsworth Longfellow 1807-1882

First Meeting – March 1970

Click, clack, click, clack. The sound of my chunky heeled boots on the recently polished parquet flooring reverberated and resounded within the confines of the long, stark corridor. The walls, having recently had a fresh lick of paint, the smell still faintly lingered. Clean and clinical. Not odious, in my view, though some would have found it unpleasant.

Increasingly, I became conscious of the sound of my heels as I was led by an officer in her sensible flat brogues, a look of disapproval, a scowl on her face. It might, however, have simply been the smell of the paint, along this first floor landing, that she was bothered by. Still, maybe I should have worn more practical shoes but fashion had, once again, ruled my head and, like always, I had given in to its demands. Anyway, I loved my new boots and had worked hard to warrant their size fives on my feet today. I tried to walk discreetly on tip-toe to deaden the sound and wondered how much further along this seemingly endless expanse of corridor the interview room would be?

We eventually arrived and, with a degree of authority, and still scowling, the officer knocked on the door. A key was turned on the inside and I stepped into the room. A carpet! Still conscious about my heels, I was relieved. Apart from the carpet, the room, just like the corridor, was stark. No faint odour of paint, however. Instead, the room was stuffy and airless. A window needed to be opened. Some fresh air needed to circulate. Already the room felt oppressive. There was little in the room by way of distraction except for a clock on the wall and a couple of nondescript paintings of flowers. The supervisory officer in attendance, about to afford us the privacy we were entitled to, made her way to stand guard outside, but not before I pointed to one of the smaller top windows. With a nod, and a cursory glance, I was granted permission to open it.

At first Angie Ross appeared like any typical, truculent teenager in trouble, sighing in an exaggerated manner to indicate how little she wanted to be involved in any real discussion. Forced, false bravado. I knew all the signs and I knew to wait.

5

I sat down on an easy chair, strategically placed by the window and opposite hers. Some attempt at creating a comfortable, less formal environment, but there was nothing at all comfortable or informal about this situation.

A coffee table separated the limited space between us and I waited. I noticed that the table, relatively new, already had a cup stain ingrained on it. Wood tarnished forever. I read once that such stains could be removed with baking soda and water. No chance of that, or time for that in this place. The stain would remain unless someone really cared and tried to restore its polished surface.

I needed to introduce myself and explain why I was there although Angie knew I was there to speak with her. She was not stupid. I already knew this much.

"Hello, Angie. My name is Susan, Susan Raynor. How are you feeling today?"

As expected, no response.

"I've been brought in so that we can talk and see if I can help you in any way. So far, I know that you haven't wanted to speak to anyone and that's okay. If you feel you still don't want to talk then we'll just sit quiet and that's fine, too."

No longer sighing, she now decided to stare. A staring game. Who would hold out the longest? I indulged her and stared back with a quiet, gentle smile on my face.

The only sound in the room was the clock's regular and consistent tick, tock, tick, tock beat. It seemed to echo and dictate further silence. Her eyes delved into mine expressionless, dead almost. There was no awkwardness. I felt as though she was looking beyond me, right through me as if I were no longer there and I knew that, behind those deep brown eyes, Angie Ross was struggling, battling with her thoughts and was lost.

The silence continued, like a healing balm, a while longer, until rudely interrupted by the pitter patter of rain on the window. The large window overlooked the recently erected units, ugly in contrast to this old, splendid building.

Steady at first, the rain started to attack the window driven by the power of the wind that had decided to blow. I looked at the small, open window above, wondering now whether to shut it but, there was no need, as the rain slid down the pane of glass and dripped, dripped away onto the green lawn below. Nature's manna, but not for me. I hated the rain. Miserable, relentless and, coupled with a blustery wind, always my enemy. A victim of fashion had its drawbacks, especially in a war between a flimsy umbrella and the elements. This enemy would definitely win today since the flimsy umbrella had been forgotten and was still at home. Drat! Hopefully, just a downpour, a shower and, when leaving, the sun would be shining just as it had done earlier in the day.

The silver birch, standing tall in the distance behind the ugly units, were so tolerant of the wind and rain. Thin, long branches, small green leaves stuck fast, intertwining but strong. These trees were planted long ago to thrive and had, so far, stood the test of time. They would continue in their glory, in their magnificence, unless cut down by man. A protected species, only to be destroyed by man's interference, if allowed, or, more likely, by man's interference if ignored.

My thoughts were brought back into the moment by another noise. Movement. Angie lifted her legs up onto the easy chair and wrapped her arms around them. The staring stopped as she now rested her head on her knees. She started to rock slowly, steadily, backwards and forwards, backwards and forwards. It was something I had seen a number of times before. A self-soothing mechanism. Backwards and forwards trying to find an escape from emotions; a release from feelings and thoughts too difficult to face. Her movements were hypnotic almost and I watched and waited and gave her time. Backwards and forwards, backwards and forwards, I continued to wait.

Outside, the deluge eased and the wind settled. The tick tock beat of the clock was once more prevalent in the room. No longer dictating further silence, it let me know that our hour together would soon be over and it nudged me to act.

"Angie? Angie?" Nothing. Backwards and forwards.

"Angie?" I tried again. "You might want to tell me about things you really like or are interested in, maybe. What do you think? Your call."

Lame, I knew that much but I had to start somewhere. I had to break the distance between us and hopefully, hopefully engage.

I tried again, "Angie?"

Suddenly, she stopped her rhythmic movement and slowly turned her head. For the first time she really looked at me. Not through me, but directly. A puzzled look, a frown almost, as if I were speaking in an alien tongue.

"Angie? Who's Angie? I'm not Angie."

She turned away. Backwards and forwards; she continued her rhythm.

Fifteen years old and she resembled someone older. Brittle, bleached blonde hair, dark roots visible. Chipped varnish on bitten down, dirty fingernails. Nasty cold sore on lips that could have been full and beautiful but, instead, were chapped and dry.

"I'm sorry. I'm sorry for getting your name wrong. What is your name?"

Reaction. The rocking stopped and she looked directly at me again.

"My name?"

"Yes, your name."

"Why? Why do you want to know my name?"

"Well, I'd like to know your name so that I can get to know you a bit better."

"A bit better? You don't know me at all so what do you mean by, a bit better? You make it sound like you already know something but want to know more."

"Is that what you think? It's just an expression. I'm sorry."

"What is it you want to know, then?"

"Whatever you'd like to tell me."

She looked at me a lot more intently now, drinking in my every feature, or so it seemed.

"I like the red," she said.

"The red?" I was puzzled.

Still hugging her knees, she managed to point a finger up towards my face.

"Yes, your lipstick. I like red lipstick."

"Oh," I smiled. "My lipstick."

I knew that young people responded more readily when they could relate to something or someone. Lipstick. It was a start.

"Yes," I continued, "it's actually called Cherry Red. I got it in Woolworths. It's Max Factor. Do you want me to show you?"

Breakthrough. She put her legs down and leaned towards me, the coffee table still a divide. She watched me closely, almost mesmerized, as I opened my handbag and got out the lipstick. She watched me closely as I lifted off the gold top and unscrewed the base to reveal the slender infusion of red. Cherry Red. A bullet of pigmentation that broke the distance between us.

"It's lovely," she said. "I used to have one just like it. My friend, Jimmy, would sometimes get it for me. He used to go to Woolworths too and get me things. I tried to tell him not to but he never listened. I wanted red lipstick, I got red lipstick. Yes, I got it."

Silence. She turned away and looked out of the window. I knew to wait until such time when she was ready to speak to me again but, for now, silence ensued.

I did not have to wait long. It was as if she had been digesting what had just taken place and had decided that I was okay. Progress. Small steps. She looked at me.

"Well?"

"Well what?" I answered softly.

11

"Well, will you be writing anything down?"

"Do you want me to write anything down?"

"Yes. Yes, I do. Like a story."

"A story? Okay."

"Right then. And, will you let me read it?"

"Of course," I answered, somewhat bemused.

"Good. I want you to use good words, proper words like they do in stories. They make things sound special."

"If that's what you want me to do," I assured her, still somewhat bemused.

"Yes, I do."

I smiled. She looked at me now up and down, up and down. I knew she was simply trying to establish in her mind whether or not she could trust me.

"You look like one of those women in the catalogues. Yes, you do. Pretty. I found a catalogue once. Someone had thrown it out with the rubbish and left it in the back street by the bin. There were newspapers there too but I wasn't interested in those. I took the catalogue. Thin, glossy colourful pages. "Empire Stores". Do you know it?"

She did not wait for an answer. Instead, with some animation, she continued her rambling.

"I'd spend ages looking through at all the lovely dresses and skirts and jumpers and shoes and boots."

She paused and pointed at my boots. "Boots like yours. Anyway, if I really liked something, sometimes I'd show Jimmy. Shouldn't have done really because then he'd go to town and see if he could get it for me or something like it. I really like those jumpers without sleeves. They look tight and snug. If I had one, I'd call it my 'hug me tight'. I liked one that was knitted in different striped colours. Have you got one? I bet you have."

Again, she did not wait for an answer.

"Yes, well, Jimmy tried to get one for me even though I told him it wasn't necessary and he didn't need to. He wanted to surprise me. Couldn't find one, though. Still, he would never come back empty handed. Even if it was just sweets or chocolate. Well, anyway, Woolworths is a magical place for sweets and chocolates. Jimmy just loved the magic! The sweets especially are all set out ready for you to help yourself and pick your own. Jimmy always did. As many as he could stuff into his pockets."

She giggled to herself, lost once more in her thoughts. She stared out of the window and silence returned enveloping the room; the tick tock beat of the clock steadily taking over.

I could not help thinking how articulate Angie Ross was for such a young girl that had missed out on so much of her education.

I broke the silence. "Did Jimmy ever manage to get you the 'hug me tight'?"

She turned her head and looked at me. Reaction.

"Pardon?"

"Jimmy? Did he ever get you the 'hug me tight', the jumper?"

No longer animated, she looked like she was going to cry and she whispered, "No. No, he didn't. Just sweets. Just some sweets."

I knew at this stage not to prompt her further as she withdrew into herself. Our session was nearly over anyway and so I began to collect my things together. The rain outside had now completely stopped. No need for my flimsy umbrella after all; the one lying abandoned in the hallway at home. Tomorrow, I must not forget it just in case.

"Jenny. My name's Jenny."

Startled, I looked at her. She was still staring out of the window.

"Sorry. What was that?"

"My name. You wanted to know my name. Well, it's Jenny. Jenny Smith."

I knew full well not to question who she said she was. Angie Ross? No, she was Jenny Smith. Dissociation with who, deep, deep down, she knew she really was.

For now, she was Jenny Smith and, as Jenny Smith, she would tell me her story.

As if she could read my thoughts she said, "Don't forget my story."

"No. No, I won't. We can start tomorrow."

"Fine, but remember you said you will write down what I tell you like a story. You know what I mean? Like in a book from a library. Yes, like in a library. I like the library. So many books and lots of peace and quiet. No-one bothers you. Libraries are wonderful places, you know. The library I go to is like a huge palace and, when you go inside, after climbing up a lot of steps, it smells all sweet. A bit like chocolate." She giggled quietly. "Maybe that's why I like it there so much…"

She was rambling animatedly again but this time I managed to interrupt. "Have you got a favourite? A favourite book?"

"A favourite book? Well, yes, there are quite a few I like and a few I have always liked from being really little. The very first book I ever tried reading by myself was all about fairies and pixies and elves and other magical beings. It was the word 'fairies', you know, that made me want to read it. A very kind man first told me about them. He didn't tell me about pixies, though, but I soon learned that they were cheeky and mischievous and enjoyed playing games under the moon. The fairies, well, they were just beautiful and magical. It was a book of poems and rhymes with lots of colourful drawings.

15

Each poem told its own little story and I loved trying to get my tongue round some of the really difficult, funny sounding words that I never understood. It didn't matter, though, because I could usually make out their meanings from all the drawings that went with them. Do you know? I can still remember the words of some of the rhymes... 'stars are shining, the moon is alight, the folk of the forest are dancing tonight..."

She paused for a brief moment, her gaze unfocused, and her thoughts, quite literally, 'away with the fairies'. Still, her flight into fancy, or distant memory, was short-lived, however, as she shook her head and looked at me.

"There is one book that will always be my favourite, though, and that's because it was the very first story that was ever read to me. It's a lovely story but sad as well. 'The Giving Tree'. Do you know it? A beautiful, very kind lady read it out loud once when I was really little. I had to ask for it in the library I go to and, even though it's for children, they still had a copy in the main library. I had to ask for it because I didn't know who had written it. All I remember is that it was a funny name. A foreign name. Anyway, this time I read it myself and I could see all the lovely drawings.

"There's a tree, you see, and it's like a mother to this little boy. A lovely mother who forgives him no matter what. As he gets older, he's always asking the tree for things and the tree, just like a good, good mother tries to give him what he wants. Sometimes, though, he's not always grateful. Whenever I read it I always imagine it's a little girl that goes to the tree. A little girl with a lovely, caring mother."

She confused me. Not only articulate but loved to read too. Probably why she was articulate.

Reading encourages a mastery of words, even picture books, when you are little, they open the mind to uncommon words. An avid reader myself, I knew this only too well and could relate to her interest in fairies and the magic of poetry and rhyme. 'The Giving Tree', however, was not a book I really knew at all. I would get a copy.

I did not want to leave. The hour had soon passed and I felt there was so much more she wanted to say. Fashion and make-up. Common ground. Books. Common ground. What else I wondered?

As I stood up I could feel her eyes following my every move. The sun started to shine through the window. So much in one hour. Blustery wind and rain and now sunshine, highlighting smears on the glass like dried up tears on a dirty face.

"What's your name again?"

A little startled I replied, "Oh, yes, of course. My name's Susan. Susan Raynor but you can call me Susie if you like."

"You don't look like you are a Susan. You look more like a… like a… like a Rose. Yes, Rose. Rosie Raynor.

Has a ring to it, don't you think? Rose for red. Red for Rose. It suits you. Yes, I like Rose."

I smiled at her. She smiled back. Some understanding. A connection of sorts. The supervisory officer, still in dutiful, stoic attendance outside the room, entered as I opened the door and informed her that the session was over.

"Right, I'll see you again tomorrow, Jenny."

"I'll see you tomorrow, Rose. Yes, I'll see you tomorrow Rosie Raynor."

From carpet to parquet flooring, I no longer cared about the click, clack of my chunky heels resonating and reverberating within the confines of the long, stark corridor ahead. In fact, I embraced the sound. Confident and wanting to make my presence felt in this austere place, I made my way back, unescorted this time, to reception.

CHAPTER 2

'Do not judge, you don't know what storm, I have asked her to walk through.'

God

January 1969

Freezing. Bleak and raw the cold tried to gnaw its way into the very core of her being. Like everything else in her life it wanted to overcome her. It wanted to beat her and leave her shivering, submitting to its icy, relentless power. She would not let it. This time nothing, no matter what, was ever going to control her or harm her. This time she had choices. Her choice now was to be firm, strong and never to be afraid again. Yes, this time choices could be made and, this time, they would be hers. All that had gone on in her life she had packed away into a huge box and wedged it to the very back of a mental cupboard. It would take quite some time for that box to be brought out and opened. Quite some time for its contents to be revealed, if ever.

After getting off the number 126, and travelling for what seemed hours, she found herself at the bus station, a bus station much the same as any other bus station in any Northern town. She would have kept on travelling but for the fact that the bus was going no further. This was its last stop before the return journey to a place she only knew as Hell. She had come this far. No going back. Ever.

She made her way across to one of the benches. She was glad the station was not busy at this time and she would have the bench to herself. Transition time between people having finished their day's labour and now at home having dinner, then getting ready to board the buses once more into town. Friday night and the station would soon be busy with happy revellers meeting friends, meeting sweethearts. A buzz of activity before the next lull.

She sat down. Plenty of room for three or, at a squeeze, four. Marked from years of scrapings and scratchings, the bench had seen better days. Initials, hearts and all the usual lacerations that no-one really took the time to read. It was almost a given that what was once pristine and unblemished just had to be ruined by mindless individuals with nothing else better to do. She leaned back on a crudely engraved communique: 'MB wuz 'ere 1962'. 1962? Who cared? She wondered for a moment whether 'MB' still sat here? If this bench was his, now that he had made his mark, or had he since claimed others around this station?

The cold continued to stalk her. She wrapped the thick, heavy coat, with its itchy fur collar, tighter around her slight frame. The coat was too big but she was glad that she had taken it. It served its purpose. The sickly, sweet smell of her mother's scent still lingered. Apart from the bottle, with its gold motif on the front, there was nothing golden about this perfume. She hated the smell and knew that, like all thoughts of her mother, it would evaporate in time. It had to.

She raised her scrawny legs up onto the bench, wrapping her arms around her knees, hugging them close, closer to her as much as she could. She rocked backwards and forwards, slowly, backwards and forwards, much the same as she had done many times before, this time trying to make sense of what she was going to do and where she was going to go. A place where she could disappear.

Her thoughts began to stray as she saw a young boy lingering not far from where she was sitting. It was only then that she also noticed her bench was positioned in between the station's public conveniences - Men's on her right and Ladies on her left. Apart from the aroma of her mother's stale perfume, she now started to smell the strong disinfectant emanating from the main doors of the toilets. Wide open doors. She liked the smell of disinfectant. It was clean, strong, clinical and mighty in its force to get rid of germs. Germs, like bad people, needed to be removed. Yes, she was somewhat comforted by the smell which gradually took precedence over her mother's scent.

The boy was a welcome distraction from her fractured thoughts. He was not very tall and, like herself, he too was thin. He had been there for some time, just as she had, and she wondered whether he was waiting for someone. A friend, maybe? His mother? His father? As she started to observe him more closely, she saw that, now and again, he would approach some man that might be walking by. One man actually stopped and went with him. They went into the toilets. Some five or so minutes later the man emerged and went on his way. The young boy came out not long after and took up a position in the same place as before.

She continued to watch him and could not help thinking how cold he must be. He did not have her mother's coat to stop him from freezing. He kept moving from foot to foot and then digging his hands deep down into his jeans' pockets; pockets not deep enough to provide any real guard against the cold. Another man walked by and the boy made his approach only this time to be shrugged away. The boy did not seem perturbed and stood by, moving from foot to foot in a vain attempt to keep warm.

Unaware that she had been staring so intently, and that the young boy had noticed, with hands still in his pockets, as deep as his jeans would allow, he came over.

"Hiya," he said.

She did not speak. She did not wish to engage in any sort of conversation with this boy and was embarrassed that he had seen her watching him so fixedly.

Close up, she could not help but notice just how young he was. Still, he could not have been much younger than herself. Eleven maybe or twelve? His face was quite rounded though the rest of him was thin and scrawny. His nose was slight and like a button and his eyes were bright and wide; a deep, deep blue. His hair was blond with soft curls just reaching his dimpled chin. He needed a haircut but nothing could detract from the fact that he was quite beautiful, like a painting that used to hang on the wall in her mother's front room. The boy in the painting was crying and, whenever she looked at it, she would wonder what had made him cry? Such a cute looking little thing. Although this boy was older and not crying, there was a cuteness, a beauty about him too that was engaging. She was staring again.

He sat down on the bench right next to her. She put her legs down and wrapped her mother's coat round her slight frame once more.

"Not seen you round here before. What's your name?"

She did not answer. She just wanted him to go away. He did not.

"My name's Jimmy. What's yours then?"

She still did not answer. Big enough hint you would think for him to just go but, instead, he carried on talking.

"Not seen you on this patch before."

'This patch?' she thought to herself. What exactly did he mean?

"I'm usually here with my friend, Will. Not here, though. Maybe he had a better offer. Still, not much business doin' tonight. Gets like that sometimes. Anyway, saw you lookin' at me. Thought I'd come over."

She remained quiet. It did not deter him.

"Yeh," he continued, "not much doin' tonight. Normally do a few more. Best time's now between six and seven since anyone wantin' anythin' knows toilets will be quiet round then. If not, then we can always go across road and over to the market. Always somewhere there but most of 'em like it here. Think it gets 'em more excited. Well, are you doin' business tonight then 'cause, like I said, not seen you before?"

Intrigued and rather confused by his words, she felt she had to answer since he was not going to leave her alone.

"Business? What do you mean, business?" she asked.

She had at last spoken and he smiled.

"Yeh, yeh, you know?"

She shook her head and did not say anything.

"Yeh, you do. Like, I give a guy a blow job, or whatever he wants, but I never do full sex. No, none of that. Yeh,

I do the business and then they pay me and that's it. Easy. I've made a few quid tonight already and only had two punters. Still, the night's young, as they say, and there's other places I can pick up later. So, what about you, then?"

"What about me?" she answered.

"What are you doin' here? Are you waitin' for someone? Are you hopin' to make a few bob too?"

She just looked at him and shrugged her shoulders. She did not know what to say and so said nothing. Silence followed and Jimmy did not seem to mind. He sat there with her and she started to welcome his presence. After all, she was a stranger in a strange place. Jimmy, young as he was, could maybe help her. She could not risk being found by the police, a possibility if she remained here alone all night sitting on a bench. The police could ask questions. They would send her back. Too soon. Much too soon. With any luck it would be days before her secret was discovered, by which time she would have disappeared, vanished. No-one would know her and no-one would ask questions. She was glad now that there were no photographs of her from where she had just come from. Her mother had always said she did not want someone ugly being on display. A couple of times at school, when photographs were taken, her mother chose not to buy them. Yes, no-one would know her in this new place.

She would often dream about a new place, a place where she would be safe and happy. The sun would always be shining. There would be rolling hills and quaint cottages with pretty flowers in the garden and garden boxes on the window ledges. She would live in one of the pretty cotton candy cottages and it would always be fresh and bright and safe. Pretty blue and white gingham curtains, tied back with silk ribbons in a bow, would hang at the small square windows. She would sit by the front window and read one of the many books lined up, straight and proud, on a shelf. All hers. A collage of stories, unique in their own way, pages and pages of creativity, ink and feeling. She loved reading.

Jimmy's voice broke her reverie and she was brought back to the station as he started to tell her more about himself. He told her that he was eleven years old and he had five brothers and a sister but did not see them anymore. He had been in care from the age of nine and, one day, he heard some of the other boys talking about being 'rent' boys. He did not have a clue what they meant. They were older than he was and used to sneak out of the care home at night in twos. It was easy. No-one really monitored them or kept a close eye on them. Once it was night time, those on duty would just make sure everyone was in their rooms, then lights out and that was it.

She turned and looked at Jimmy who had confided so much already in someone he had never met before and she wondered why? He was quiet for a moment, lost in his thoughts. He was so young. December 6th, and she had just turned fourteen, not much older than Jimmy, yet she felt decidedly older. What he had told her did not shock her at all. Nothing could anymore. So far remaining quiet and unresponsive, she was the one now to speak.

"Why are you telling me all this? You don't even know me."

"Why?"

She nodded.

"Why? Because you look so sad and you're so pretty. You shouldn't be sad. I just want to let you know about me. Anyway, just talkin' makes me feel good. I don't really get a chance to talk to anyone proper like, well, at least to anyone that'll listen."

No-one had ever called her pretty before except for one person whose words, she soon discovered, were empty and meant nothing. Nothing at all. She had always thought she was ugly and dirty and hideous. Not pretty at all. She started to warm a little to this young boy who seemed to like her and so she spoke again. She was curious.

"What did you mean? Lights out and that was it?"

"Oh, yeh. Well, those stupid bastards, supposed to be supervisin' us, would go and watch TV in the staffroom, smoke their fags, drink tea, eat biscuits and then fall asleep. That's when they'd sneak out. The 'rent boys'. They'd sneak through the window and go and make some money. They made lots of it and went and got fags and booze and anythin' else they wanted. It was easy and I wanted in. I wanted to buy fags and booze and other things too."

She had never before heard of 'rent boys'.

"What do you mean, 'rent boys'?" she asked.

"Yeh," he said, "I d'int know either but then I found out that all they had to do was give a guy a blow job and then they got money. Some of 'em even had full sex and let the guy put it up 'em. Only the really desperate ones though 'cause they got a lot more money doin' that. Not me. Pull it, suck it, nothin' else.

"I'd not been in the home a year when I persuaded 'em to let me go too. Of us all, I were the youngest. The others were all between ten and fifteen. I were nearly ten. There were about seven of us. The first one I did was a fella called Joe. He become a regular but now he's dead. Got beaten really bad one night by these guys. Shame really 'cause he were always easy. I only had to look at him and he'd be comin' in his pants. Anyways, at first, I d'int like it but, when money was handed over, it seemed worth it. I got to like it.

"I don't live at that care home anymore. I 'aven't for ages. I ran away. I'm still on the run but they'll never find me. Police don't care. They've other things to do. I live with Will now and a few other lads in a squat. It's our squat and we look out for each other. Where do 'you' live?"

A stress on the word 'you' suggested that, since Jimmy had told her about himself, she should return his confidence and tell him something about her.

"I don't live anywhere. I'm new here and don't know anywhere yet."

"Are you a runaway, too?"

She nodded and hung her head. She hoped he would get the hint and stop pushing for answers. She guessed all runaways had a story to tell but they were their stories until such time as they were ready to share them. She was not ready. She looked at Jimmy whose cherub profile now stared straight ahead as if looking at some distant place far removed from this concrete, miserable station. He was quiet and she could not help thinking was it really just the money that made him do what he did? No-one was forcing him. It had to be something else and she knew, she realised that, like herself, Jimmy was a by-product, a left-over of a ruined childhood and that, through choice, he had not told her his full story, just the part he was happy with.

Jimmy stood up. "Right, come on then. Let's find you somewhere to stay."

"Somewhere to stay?"

"Yeh, that's right."

As the cold was becoming more and more hostile, licking at her face and trying to creep under her clothes, stiff-limbed, she got up from the bench. With teeth starting to chatter, she wrapped her mother's coat around her, the sickly, sweet aroma still lingering, and followed her new friend.

They left the bus station. As they crossed over the road her eyes were immediately drawn to a magnificent building. It was fairytale with its neon lights enhancing the green and black tiles trimming its cream facade. She counted six tall windows in the centre and above. This was the Odeon cinema; its bold letters proudly lighting up the night sky. She had only ever been to a cinema once. Her class had been taken there as a treat when she was little and she remembered the joy it brought her. Every moment was pure escapism that tickled her love of reading to the next level. She had read some of the 'Wizard of Oz' but now the film allowed her to be Dorothy in full technicolour triumph. Seeing this palace of film, just knowing it was there, lifted her spirits. A go to place where she could be the main character and there would always be a 'happy ever after'.

Heavy rain decided now to join forces with the bitter cold wind. Steadfast in their attack, she found it difficult to focus on anything else around her as she tried to keep in step with Jimmy's quickening pace, his thin legs, like pistons, never faltering once. She tucked her head down close to her chin and, hair whipping round her face, she did not look up again. As soon as she was able she would cut her hair short. This was something she knew she must do anyway.

Bracing her head against the wind and rain, she thought about the Friday night revellers going into town. She did not envy them. The evening was one to stay indoors by the fire, read a book, eat cake and drink tea or hot chocolate. A story book scenario she had often wished for.

With her head still bent down, the pavement soon became her only focus, almost hypnotising with each quickening step taken to reach wherever it was they were going. In order to remain focused, she found herself trying not to stand on a nick in the pavement, remembering the old rhyme in her head: 'If you stand on a nick, you'll marry a stick and a beetle will come to your wedding'. Inevitably, you would find yourself walking quicker in an attempt to avoid the pavement cracks but the wind and rain even made that difficult now. It was something she would do on her way home from school. Not that she wanted to hurry home, she only wanted to believe that, if she could avoid all the nicks more and more, then the rest of her life would be beautiful. Not filled with beetles. A silly rhyme and a silly game and she knew it was not real. She was good at avoiding the nicks, the cracks in the pavements, but her life just got worse. Beetle, after beetle, after beetle. Still, she carried on in her head, 'If you stand on a... If you stand on a... If you stand on a ...' until, before she knew it, Jimmy interrupted her rhythmic beat.

"Slow down. We're nearly there," he said

Without realising, she had started to walk ahead of him, lost, lost in concentration. She must have looked quite ridiculous in her hastening staccato movement on the pavement. Jimmy had not seemed to notice, just that she was leaving him a little behind.

She now looked up and took stock of where they were. Thankfully, the rain had started to ease somewhat but it was still windy and cold. Hair now plastered and dripping down her face, she was annoyed that, in her haste to leave Hell, she could not bring herself to return to her room and tie it back.

Although it seemed that they had been walking forever, Jimmy told her they were not that far away from the town and the house was close by in Beacon Street.

Beacon Street? Beacon? She recalled reading somewhere about a person being a 'beacon of hope', steering someone through the darkness. A 'beacon', a bright light or a warning? She wondered at the irony of the name and which one of these row upon row of houses would be Beacon Street? They all looked the same. A warren of gloom was what she observed now, devoid of any brightness or hope. No pretty cotton candy houses here and no pretty blue and white gingham curtains tied back with silk ribbons.

Lamp posts cast their glow over the terraces; the private lives of its inhabitants shielded by drab, drawn curtains. As Jimmy took her down the back of one of these sad, military rows, she felt uncomfortably close to the contagious stretch of premises. She heard water gushing into grates, the dropping of a pail outside a back door, the banging of another door and the sound of voices. From one house a child was screaming and voices were raised. So many houses cheek to jowl, so many squirming lives, so many backyards. Maybe, just maybe, there would be no beetles here. After all, she had avoided the nicks in the pavements but, somehow, somehow she knew that these streets probably housed their fair share of them and in more ways than one.

Jimmy opened the back gate of one of these houses and immediately a foul, rotten stench hit her. The bin inside the yard was full, its lid perched precariously on a mound of rubbish. There was an outside toilet. She saw it since the door was no longer there but leaning up against a wall.

Jimmy knocked a rat a tat, tat on the back door and walked straight inside. He motioned her to follow. She stepped into the kitchen, a mere box of a room and, just like the outside, it was smelly and grimy. The light was on and she could see that the sink was still full of dirty water with dishes and crockery floating in a film of grease.

As they went through to the next room she tried not to focus on any of the negatives. A standard lamp was switched on in the corner of the room and she was heartened to see a gas fire, with dancing uniform flames safe behind its iron grille, creating a warm glow and

making this equally untidy room a lot more inviting. She
had forgotten, for a moment, how cold she had been
and started to loosen the hold on her mother's coat.

Jimmy called out, "Alice? Alice? It's me. Jimmy.
Brought someone to see you."

She heard a slow shuffling coming from the front room.
She did not know what to expect and felt nervous. Alice
eventually appeared and straightaway posed a dominant
presence. She was big and flabby and shuffled since her
weight made movement difficult. Every step seemed to
render breathlessness. She was grubby and her bleached
blonde hair had seen better days. Some attempt at
prettying herself had been made, though not very well.
Bright orange lipstick had been applied to her thin,
puckered lips. A gaudy and garish colour that did not
suit her at all. Her eyes were lost in the folds of her
cheeks but some attempt had been made on those too.
A smudge of bright blue on each lid and, above those, a
line of black, arched to try and create a semblance of
brows that had been plucked to almost nothing.

Alice sat down. Squeezing her bulky frame into the
armchair by the fire, she stretched out her legs and the
sour, acrid smell of her feet soon began to permeate the
already stale air.

Looking at Alice now, she could not determine any real
age. Forty perhaps? Maybe not even that. Jimmy
seemed at home in this hovel and appeared at ease with
the smell. She made a conscious effort to smile politely,
letting her hair fall over her nose to discreetly block the

smell and, all the while, glancing towards the door checking her exit was clear. She wanted to run but, with hardly any money left in the pocket of her mother's coat, and nowhere else to go, she knew she would be staying.

"Alright then, Jimmy lad. Who's this then?"

Alice's voice was raspy. Years of heavy smoking no doubt and she was not surprised to see a packet of Park Drive on the mantle shelf. Strong tobacco. She knew someone else who had favoured the brand and admonished herself for letting that memory slip from its mental cupboard.

Alice looked at her up and down, seemingly nodding in approval. She suddenly felt naked as if every part of her young body was exposed for scrutinization.

"Well?" asked Alice.

"This, this is? Do you know?" he said, "I 'aven't a clue! She's not told me yet." He started laughing.

She had to think quickly. She did not have time to start going through the alphabet and dawdling over names beginning with each of the letters, something she would do when she wanted to escape reality and numb herself to the torture of Hell. No. She had to think fast and blurted out a name she had always liked. It was the name of someone in her class - the pretty, popular girl who was everything she was not.

"Er...it's Jenny. My name's Jenny."

"There you go, Alice. It's Jenny. She's called Jenny."

"Thanks, Jimmy. I'm not bloody deaf, you know!"

Jimmy laughed again.

"Well, what do you want?" she asked.

"Well, I were thinkin', Alice. Jenny's new here in town and has nowhere to go. Found her on the Lane and I thought I know someone that might have a room goin' since Emma's done a runner. Think she'll be okay here."

She listened somewhat confused. 'Okay? Okay for what?' she wondered.

"Yeh," Alice replied, "the stupid bitch. Left me right in the shit! I've had to drag Shirl off Spa Street to take care of Emma's lot but Shirl prefers it on the street. Most of 'em do. Don't get as much doin' it from here. Still, Shirl's no choice. Owes me big time."

She looked at her up and down again, "Yeh, you could be right, Jimmy. She's young and pretty. They like 'em young. How old are you and don't lie?"

In Alice's formidable, smelly presence she knew there was no point in lying. "I'm fourteen," she said, "just turned."

"Okay, and have you started your monthlies yet?"

Again, she was confused. "My monthlies?" she asked.

"Yeh, you know? Your periods?"

Still confused, she had to ask again, "My periods?"

Alice tutted. "Yeh, your periods. Do you bleed down there every month?" She motioned and pointed between her legs.

She could only ever remember bleeding 'down there' once and that was a long, long time ago. Only recently she had bled from somewhere else 'down there' but somehow, she knew that this was not where Alice meant. That memory was right at the bottom of the box in her mental cupboard. Yes, right at the bottom.

 "Well, do you?"

"No," she answered

"Good," Alice said, "no chance of any little accidents. Well, not yet anyway. As soon as you bleed you'll let me know won't you?"

She gestured acknowledgement but still very much baffled.

Alice continued, "Yeh, Jimmy. They'll be likin' her alright. You've told her, haven't you?"

Jimmy nodded. "I think she's got it. I found her on the bench near the toilets and she'd been there ages. Business has been really slow tonight. Must be the cold. Enough to freeze your bollocks off!"

Alice smirked. "Listen," she said, "Jimmy'll get you some makeup and stuff tomorrow. Whatever you'll be needin' for the job. Won't you, Jimmy? We want you lookin' your best."

Jimmy nodded eagerly.

She was confused and, with brow creased and face tense, she asked, "What job?"

At this Alice laughed out loud. "What job? What bloody job? You don't think you can stay here for free, do you? No. You have to bloody well earn your keep. Men'll come and I'll take some of what they give me for you. Yeh, you'll get a cut and I'll take rest."

Alice paused for a moment and then, frowning, she asked, "Nobody knows you're here do they? Don't want any trouble comin' to this place. Well?"

She shook her head, "No. There's no-one that knows me or knows I'm here."

Alice was satisfied. "Okay. Right. Well then, startin' Monday, you can go out at 4 o' clock. That's when schools are out and you'll just look like any other kid that's been home, got changed and gone back into town. You can do what you like so long as you get back here no later than 7 o' clock so as you can get yourself ready to start. First one'll probably come just after 8 o'clock and then you'll be workin' right through with breaks in between. Tend to just get our regulars but they pay okay and, who knows, might get some others if they find out we've got someone new. Weekends can get busy. It all depends.

"Yeh, Jimmy. You're right. Tonight's been slow. Bloody weather's kept a lot of the sad bastards indoors. Prefer their poor bloody wives and girlfriends or just theirselves rather than comin' out in this.

"Anyway, Shirl can finish the weekend here. She can use my room then Monday she can go back on the street to work. Yeh, you can have some time to get yourself sorted but it'll mean you won't get paid for your first couple of nights when you do start. Get yourself settled into your room, and that, and then you'll be able to give clients what they want. Alright?"

Like the cat that got the cream and more, Alice's gaudy orange lips were almost licking as she paused once more and the impact of her words started to fully dawn. She recalled Jimmy telling her about 'business' and now understood that to Jimmy, anyone hanging around a bus station on their own at night, must be part of his dark world, a world where favours are sold. To Jimmy, it was a way of life. Nothing unusual.

Alice's raspy voice sounded once more, "You've had sex before, haven't you?"

There was nothing stopping her from getting out, nothing stopping her from leaving. Absolutely nothing and no-one at all. She was free to go and she had a choice to make. Her choice right now was to nod her head and stay. After all, it could not be any worse than what she had been made to endure before. This time would be different, though. This time she would be the one in control of her actions. She was a big girl now and, this time, she would own it.

Alice looked at her and smiled. "Right," she said, "Shirl's just finishing now. That'll be Ronnie comin' downstairs. Give us a few minutes and then, Jimmy, you can show Jenny to the room and sort out all she'll be wantin' or needin'. Room's all yours.

"Ron? Ronnie! Wait up. Somethin' to tell you about for next time."

Alice heaved herself up from the chair, the rolls of fat and flab wobbling and shuffling away. A stomach-churning mix of smelly feet, stale dirt and grease hung in her wake.

CHAPTER 3

'Life is not a matter of holding good cards but
sometimes playing a poor hand well.'

Jack London 1876 – 1916

Jenny

She had a roof over her head at least. All she had to do
now was what she had been forced to do for as long as
she could remember. This time, though, she was not
being forced. This time she was Jenny and Jenny had
agreed. Consenting to an act she would be getting
money for, she would use this to her advantage. If she
could save up enough then, one day, she could go and
live in the cotton candy house that often filled her
dreams. Sitting on the wooden chair in the corner of the
room, she held on to this as she recalled the night's
events …

Soon after Alice had left, and hurried footsteps down the stairs had signalled Shirl's departure, Jimmy took her to the room. She tried not to register too closely the dark, gloomy stairwell and the sticky, worn carpet beneath her feet. Jimmy escorted her like some proud estate agent selling a brand new, upmarket dwelling, his cheeky, cherub smile a permanent fixture.

It was a back room. Jimmy switched on the light. A naked bulb hanging from the ceiling cast a dull, soulless glare and added to the misery of what she now observed. A double bed took up most of the limited space and, apart from a single wardrobe, chest of drawers and a small wooden chair that was in the corner by the window, there was room for little else. No ornaments, no pictures, nothing at all. No fripperies. The slow creep of time and neglect had left its mark. Damp, dirty walls held the cold inside the room like a firm friend. A single sash window overlooked the yard and, as she went over to glance out, its twin, across the narrow back street, seemed a little too close for comfort. She tried to draw the curtains. Thin and a dirty grey with one side partly hanging down, these curtains afforded only a tiny measure of privacy. There was no sticky carpet, just floorboards and a rough, worn rug by the bed. Despite the grittiness she could feel beneath her shoes, she was relieved since floorboards could be swept and scrubbed clean. The walls too, since they were bare, could be saved with a good clean.

Already, she had not been in the room for more than a couple of minutes and she was making it her own. A space where, regardless of what the rest of the house was like and, regardless of what her night time work would entail, in the light of each new day her time in this room would be unsullied and quiet and she would make it as cotton candy as she could. Two separate entities - day and night, night and day.

Jimmy came over and nudged her. "Well? What do you think? Alice said you can do what you want with it. So long as you make your money at night, she's not bothered."

She did not say anything and, for a few more silent moments, they stood side by side until she went and sat down on the wooden chair in the corner. She looked at her little friend with his blond curls and cute smile. So eager to please. He went and sat down on the unmade bed, its grubby sheets still warm from work no doubt. His head nodding, anticipating approval, Jimmy asked again, "What do you think? Will it do?"

She tried her best to smile, not wanting to dampen his enthusiasm. "Yes," she said, "it's fine, but it needs cleaning and I shall be wanting to do a few things. Did Alice really mean it when she said I can do what I want? I have hardly any money left so how can I?"

She knew that she would be earning money soon enough but she wanted to start making changes straight away. She did not want to be in this filth for too long. She found it suffocating and it frightened her. A room like this would bring disquiet. A room like this meant a lack of control and control was needed. Control was crucial.

Jimmy must have seen a look of concern painfully starting to etch itself across her face and he wanted to reassure her. "Don't worry," he said. "Listen, I can get you whatever you want and you won't have to pay. Makeup and that, Alice said to get you anyhow and they're easy to lift. Never paid for anythin' ever except for some things."

She wondered what he actually spent money on and, as if reading her thoughts, he went on to explain.

"Yeh, there are some things I need money for like proper grub. You know, like pasties and pies and stuff from the chippy. There's an old pasty shop in town and the pasties and pies and cakes are so yummy but they're all behind a counter. Anyway, the woman as owns it is really nice and calls me cheeky. 'Hello cheeky,' she says, and, 'what can we do for you today?' And, a lot of the time, she gives me little extras. Yeh, love it there. She's called Mavis. I call her Aunty Mavis. She always smiles and laughs and that's why she calls me cheeky. Chippy's same. You can't nick anythin' from there 'cause that's all behind a counter too. Mmm chippy dinner or chippy tea, depends when you're wantin' it. Bloody lovely!

"And then, there's horses and the dogs. I like puttin' a bet on 'em but got to get one of the older lads to do that for me. And then, there's cards. Troy, he's Jamaican, he runs a card school and lets me and some of the other rent lads in. Doesn't really let any other white people in except us 'cause we're okay and he knows we won't grass 'cause he'd get banged up if he got caught. Not legal these card places. He has a back room as well. He thinks we don't know but we do. It's private and he does let some of the richer white guys from round here in there but that's big, big money. Anyway, we play poker and he takes ten percent of the stake and, if we want booze, we can buy that there too. I hardly ever win though and same on the dogs and horses. One day, you know, I'll win it all back and more and then I'll go and live in a mansion and you can come too if you want."

She smiled. Jimmy had his dreams too. "Thanks," she said. "Anyway, it's not just the makeup, and what Alice has said I'll need, it's other things too."

"That's okay. Like what?"

"Well, I'll be wanting to do things in the room. I want to make it clean and a bit brighter."

Jimmy didn't seem fazed. "Right, that's okay. Don't worry. You just tell me what you want, Jen."

It was the first time Jimmy had used her new name, or at least his endearment of it, and it took her a second or two to register that he was actually addressing her. It suddenly dawned on her just how much had happened since waking up and to where she was now - making decisions on how to change a room. She warmed to Jimmy even more. Without him she would have probably been still sitting on a bench, alone and lost with no direction. Maybe there was a God, after all, and he had sent Jimmy. So far, he had not answered any of her prayers or any of her questions. Maybe this was an answer. Maybe most girls let men invade them. Maybe that is what most girls were made for. Maybe the man from Hell had been telling her the truth. But then, maybe all men were not the same and some were kinder than others. Anyway, Jimmy had been sent at a time when she needed him and she knew he would do whatever he could for her. She trusted him and, for the first time, she said his name too. They were friends.

"Jimmy? Why are you doing all this for me? I have nothing I can give you."

"Give me? I don't want anythin'. Like I said before, when we were on the Lane, you know, the bus station, you looked so sad and you don't have to be. You shouldn't be. I want you to be a friend. I know I've got Will but he's not always a good friend. He can get really moody and then turns really mean and nasty and then he gets mad, which is a lot of the time. When he gets like that he beats me up. Don't really hurt me, though. I can take it. You look like you need a friend and I can look after you." He chuckled. "Anyway, I don't think you'd ever give me a beating. You look like you couldn't even flatten a flea."

She winced inside but tried to affect a smile. She felt Jimmy needed her to smile and the reassurance that he was helping her in his way.

"Well then," he said, "let me know what you want and tomorrow, first thing, I'll go to town and see what I can get."

She knew how to clean. She had been made to scrub and dust and polish and keep things tidy from being very little and always afraid that, if it was not up to standard, she would get a slap. Her fear had made her resourceful, more than capable

"Bleach," she said. "I'll need bleach and, if you can, some disinfectant."

"Bleach? What do you want bleach for?"

"It's for cleaning the floor and the walls too. I'll also need washing up liquid. That's good mixed with bleach to make things clean. It also goes a long way. It's good for all sorts and not just dishes."

"Right, then. Bleach and dis… dis… disintetant and washin' up stuff. Yeh, That's easy. Anythin' else?"

She shook her head slowly. Rhyming off, one thing after another, as she had been doing, made her feel guilty. She had never dared ask for anything before in her life. She had never been allowed. Asking now felt strange and foreign

"So, bleach, cleanin' stuff. Okay, I won't forget," Jimmy assured her. "I can get it all at market and then there's always Woolies. Saturday, so town's going to be busy. That's good. Will can help. He's good at liftin' too. He'll just enjoy the thrill and, if he gets chased, all the better.

47

No-one's ever caught him. He's quick. Once he nicked a whole row of shoes on a rack outside Dolcis. They were there all in rows so he bundled 'em up and ran all the way down the high street. Silly sod. Only realised later that they were all right feet. No use to anyone. Bloody funny. Couldn't stop laughin'.

"Yeh, Will'll help and bring stuff back here, too. He won't come in, though. Frightened to death of Alice. Calls her Fat Alice and she doesn't like him much either. Anyway, market'll be easy. Lots of stalls. People everywhere. There's everythin' there like I said. So, are you sure there's nothin' else you'll be wantin'?"

She thought for a moment, "Erm, do you think Alice might have a sweeping brush somewhere?"

Jimmy laughed, "'Course she will. Probably never used it much, though. Well, maybe when she could move around a bit easier she mighta done. It's probably in the kitchen or out in the backyard. I'll take a look for you before I go. I know she's got a bucket in the yard. I've kicked it a few times."

He started laughing again, this time at his own joke, "Kicked bucket - do you get it?"

She could not help but chuckle. Jimmy's happy vibrancy was infectious, like a tickle, and she felt encouraged to ask for a few more things if he could manage it. She did not cherish the thought of having to sleep on the bed with its crumpled sheets and pillow cases, nor did she really want to wash them. These sheets and cases held history and she wanted new. She asked Jimmy whether it would be a problem. He shook his head and added 'bed stuff' to his memory list.

There was one last thing she wanted to know and, despite having requested so much already, she had to find out. She wondered whether the market would have material so that she could do the window a favour and put up new curtains. She could already see herself cutting the material into two pieces and, with some safety pins, she could somehow fold the top of the material loosely around the pole and pin along and make do. The window was not large which meant, if there was enough material, she could double the pieces and so afford more insulation and privacy. She even thought she could tie them back with string or cuts of leftover material. Her imagination, as ever, was coming to her aid and she was thankful. She even described what gingham looked like - small checks and that blue and white would be nice.

Still smiling and nodding, Jimmy added material to his memory list, safety pins included. "No probs., like I were sayin', market has everythin'. Seen rolls of material and stuff there. If we can't find that blue and white thingy we'll get what we can. We'll bring everythin' back here first but we'll have to go back for the material and one of us'll just lift it and do a runner. Yeh, easy."

"Jimmy? Do you think Alice will have a pair of scissors that I could use?"

"'Course she will. You can ask her yourself you know. She won't bite. I know she can be a bit frightenin' at first but that's 'cause she's so bloody fat and wants everyone to think she'll bloody well kill 'em if they try to take advantage or get on the wrong side of her. She likes me, though. I'm her little helper, she says. She sleeps in the front bedroom but spends most of her time in the front room downstairs. You want to see it."

She thought straightaway that, no, she did not want to see it if what she had seen so far was anything to go by. Still, she knew she would have to see Alice anyhow. She needed the scissors and not just for the material. She also wanted to cut her hair. She thought about bleaching it too. Anything to change her appearance, just in case. Alice bleached hers, that much was obvious, not very well but still she would know what to use

"Jen? Got to get you some makeup don't forget. Do you want lipstick like Alice's?"

She was quick to answer, "No! Not like Alice's."

She recalled a beautiful lady who was once so kind to her when she was little. A gentle, pretty lady who wore red lipstick and who had taught her so much.

"Red lipstick, Jimmy," she said, "I'm not really bothered about anything else. As long as I have the red lipstick, that will be enough."

"What about clothes?" Jimmy asked

"Clothes?"

"Yeh, you'll be needin' somethin'. You've only got jeans and your coat. You're probably wearin' a jumper as well. Don't know. Can't really see. Anyway, you can't be wearin' those. So, what do you think?"

"I don't know. I can't really think," she answered. Clothes were the last thing on her mind. At least everything she was wearing now was clean. She had made sure of that.

"Okay then. Don't worry. I'll ask Alice. She'll know."

She was not sure about that but, for now, she would have to trust in Alice's judgement.

"Right then, best be off. I'll see Alice on my way out. It's not too late either, you know, to see what I can do in the park before I go back. Squat's not far from here and park's only up road. Park's a good hang out for fellas wanting somethin' late on. Can make a few more bob if I'm lucky. 'Lucky Jim' that's me." He was laughing again.

'Lucky?', she thought to herself, and she suddenly felt protective. "Okay, Jimmy, but listen. Be careful."

"'Course I will. Anyway, see you first thing. I'll be early."

"Early?"

"Yeh, as soon as shops open me and Will'll be out. Like I said, Saturday's always a busy day so that's good.

We've got lots to get and I know you'll be wantin' to make a start."

"Jimmy?"

"Yeh?"

"Thank you."

Smiling, a total picture of impish innocence, Jimmy left the room shutting the door quietly behind him.

Outside, the rain had ceased and the wind had died down in its attack on the town. The cold's icy fingers though were still trying to take hold of her and she was stirred into action. She looked up at the naked bulb hanging from the ceiling, no shade to soften its joyless glow. A lamp would be better. Maybe Alice might have one somewhere, one that could be salvaged amongst the debris of the house.

She looked over at the bed, not relishing the thought of lying down but knew she had to eventually. She was tired, very tired and now, in the aftermath of all that had gone on previously, sleep started to force itself upon her.

Wearily, she got up from the chair, wrapping her mother's coat tightly round her skinny frame once more, and went to switch off the light. After a split second of pitch black her eyes gradually adjusted to the room's shadowy darkness. She walked over to the bed and lay down uneasily, trying so hard not to breathe in the stale stench of sweat and bodies firmly fixed into the sheets' grubby fibres. Lifting the coat collar further up round her face, the sickly, sweet smell of her mother's perfume trapped in the itchy fur disguised, for a time, evidence of the night's drama played out on this iniquitous platform.

It would very soon be her platform. She knew that, and she would be directing the script. It did not frighten her. It did not unsettle her. After all, she reminded herself, it would be no different to what she had become used to on so many levels but, this time, she would be the principal director leading the sad individuals, acting as men, and doing what men did to girls. This time, as long as she was directing, then, all the performances to come would just blend into one.

She looked up at the ceiling, with its shadowy outline of stains and dirt, wishing that they were stars and that God, in his heaven would give her an answer to the question that forever tortured her mind. Why had she been singled out to suffer from the minute she had been born?

No matter how many times she asked, answers never came. She was determined to make the most of the dark void before her refusing to let it dig deep into her soul and swallow all her hopes and dreams. She knew how to switch off. She had become an expert but, should that ever become impossible again, she knew she would, and could, do something about it. With this resolve in mind, she closed her eyes and, at last, surrendered to the silence and quiet of sleep.

CHAPTER 4

'Let us not look forward in fear but around us in
awareness.'

James Thurber 1894-1961

January 1969

'He smiles and beckons her to come. "Follow me," he
says. "Come. Follow me." He is an angel, a beautiful
angel dressed in white. She wraps her blood-stained
fingers round his hand, her heart gushing with relief.
She could walk through the dark forest on her own she
supposed but it is wonderful to have a guide.

He leads her through the dark forest. The blood on her
fingers, sticky and congealed, are still wrapped around
his hand. The forest is dark, very dark, so very dark and
he leads her through. He leads. She follows. He leads.
She follows, longing to get through the darkness and
look up at the bright coloured rainbow blotches in the
sky so full of grace and happiness and...'

A loud clattering and uncontrollable giggling and laughter made her jump. For a moment she wondered where she was but, as sunlight tried to shine its way through the frail film of dirty curtains, one side half hanging down, reality registered making her gasp. Every thought now in high definition, she knew that she must have slept for too long. She had wanted to be up early. The giggling and laughter, outside in the backyard, could only be Jimmy and Will returning from their early morning shopping spree. Her thoughts now gathering, she recalled the things she had asked for and suddenly felt excited. She would not allow herself to feel guilty. She let herself think, there and then, that it was not really stealing. It was borrowing. The only difference being it would never be given back.

To recompense, she quickly decided that, once she had some money of her own, she would go to the market, and into the town, and buy things for herself and so give back in her own way.

Still, she knew Jimmy enjoyed his pilfering jaunts and she knew he wanted to please her. That much had been clearly established not long after they had first met at the bus station just the night before. He had no hidden agenda. He just wanted a friend.

She had to get up and knew that, after lying in the same position for so long, moving suddenly would prove painful. She counted slowly – one, two, three and up. The frigid air straightaway penetrated her skin and, once again, thankful for her mother's coat, she wrapped it tightly round her, unwilling to concede to the bitter cold now firmly trapped in the room. Eventually, when she herself could get something more substantial, a warm coat of her own, she would abandon this one. She hated it. She loathed it. She wanted to burn it. Until such time, however, her mother's coat was preferable to freezing to death.

She made her way to the window and carefully drew open the half hanging apology for curtains. The condensation had left pools on the peeling ledge and, reluctantly, she wiped the window with her hand, its cruel iciness numbing her fingers at first touch. The disturbed condensation started to trickle slowly down in tiny waves distorting, for a time, what Jenny could see on the other side. There was no mistaking, though, that it was Jimmy at least in the backyard since, no longer laughing and giggling, she could still hear him pottering about.

She knocked on the window. Jimmy came into view and raised his head. He was smiling and gave her a thumbs up. She could not quite grasp how happy she was to see him. Happiness was an emotion she rarely experienced and it felt strange yet warming.

Jimmy shouted, "Alright to come up?"

She nodded her head vigorously, not sure whether he could see her through the waves of dirty condensation. She could not wait to give the window a clean

Jimmy had seen her and, within seconds, he appeared breathless outside her room. "Alright to come in?" he shouted. Nothing quiet about Jimmy.

She smiled and called out, "Yes, come in."

With arms full of recent acquisitions, he blundered into the room depositing what he was carrying onto the floor.

"Here. Not done yet. Couldn't bring it all up at once. Back in a jiffy."

Her eyes could not quite believe what was in front of her. A proper hoard. Already she liked what she saw but, before she touched anything, she wanted to wait for Jimmy to return and let him show her himself. For some reason, she felt it would spoil a moment for him. She had sensed his excitement and the liquid sunshine bursting from within his soul. It just made her want to smile. She could not believe that she was smiling once more. She never thought she could smile and certainly not now after what she had done. There was never any reason to smile. But, that was then, this was now. Now, she was Jenny, Jenny Smith. Yes, Jenny Smith. Smith, as good and ordinary a surname as any and, right now, Jenny Smith wanted to smile. Yesterday, and all the days before, were in the box, the one set back in the deepest recesses of her mental cupboard and the door was locked. Padlocked.

Jenny Smith was here and, for now, Jenny was here to stay.

She heard Jimmy's hurried footsteps on the stairs and awaited another exuberant entrance. Jenny was not disappointed. He bounded in beaming with satisfaction. He was holding a roll of material. Not gingham but a pretty flowery pattern of pastel pinks and blues.

"I know, I know," he sighed. "It's not that gingy stuff you said but couldn't see any of that. Saw this, though, and thought it were pretty, just like you. So, there you go. It's a match." He giggled and Jenny started giggling too. Again, he had said she was pretty. What could he see, she wondered, that she could not?

Nodding he said, "Well, do you like it?"

"Yes, Jimmy. I love it. I really do."

Jimmy was delighted. "Right," he said, "show you what we got then."

Jenny watched as he knelt down and quickly started to unravel the heap that had been left on the floor. "Okay. Bleach, washin' up liquid…" He held up each item before placing it on the bed. In the same vein he continued to hold up for inspection the rest of his plunder.

"Even got disi… disi… disintetant. Didn't really know what to look for but thought it would be on the bleach stall and that. So, I asked this woman if she could see any. She started laughin'. Don't know why. Anyway, she pointed me to some."

Jenny was tempted to correct his mispronunciation but felt it unfair to do so. He had done well in his mission so far and she wanted him to know how thankful she was.

"Got you some pins as well. Will says they're nappy pins. Not a clue what that means but look – they've even got blue tops. They'll match the curtains, you know, the little blue flowers in 'em.

"I've brought bucket in from the yard and left it in the kitchen. There's a brush there too and a mop. Mop's in the bucket." He stopped speaking and stared at Jenny, beaming as usual.

Jenny sensed that he was building up to saying something of magnitude. Well, to him at least.

"And last, we got these!" he exclaimed. He lifted up an old, tatty shopping bag. Jenny could feel his delight and knew that, whatever she thought about its contents, she would feign absolute pleasure so as not to dampen his joy

Nodding his head, Jimmy could not wait to show her. In a cellophane wrapped package was a double sheet and pillow cases. She looked in awe at her Artful Dodger as he produced another two similar packages. "Yeh, I got this first and Will said one's not enough and he went and grabbed a couple more. He's even gone back for you. Said you'll be needin' new blankets too and he knows where he can easily lift some. Don't worry, there's lots of stalls and we never go back to the same ones on the same day. There's lots of stalls selling same things. Anyway, Will says he's had a great day. A game of see it, grab it, run for it! Yeah, great fun! So, what do you think?"

Jenny was dumbstruck. Jimmy's energy was quite breathtaking and, for a minute, she was lost for words. Jimmy had little sense of right and wrong and, as she looked at his beautiful deep, deep blue eyes staring at her and awaiting approval, it was not the colour or the shape that she saw but the loving, sweet essence that was so clearly there. Jenny knew that she had found an angel.

"Thanks ever so much, Jimmy. Everything, everything is perfect."

"'Honestly?"

"Yes, honestly," she assured him

"Oh good," he sang, giving away another one of his cheeky cherub smiles like a wish.

There was pure mischief in his eyes now as he put his hand into his pocket and slowly, and deliberately, as if performing some magic trick, he said, "And, that's not all." He paused. A dramatic pause, and, with much glee, he revealed a huge bar of Cadbury's Dairy Milk chocolate. "Thought you might be starvin' by now. What do you think?"

His question seemed absurd. What did she think? Chocolate. Chocolate was gold. It had helped Jenny for years to escape the hunger that would gnaw at her stomach when there was not any food. She adored the velvety, rich smoothness of creamy, melting sweetness. Bliss. In Hell chocolate was her heaven. It was always an easier option when meals were rarely prepared or given and real food was just not there. At least at school she always had lunch to look forward to and it often was the only proper meal she had in a day. Right now, she was almost salivating. It suddenly dawned on her that, apart from a measly portion of cereal and a cup of water, the previous afternoon in her hurry to leave, she had not had anything to eat at all. Her body had become so accustomed to the pangs of hunger and her stomach was often empty. She had learned to bear with the sinking emptiness but, when presented with paradise in a bar, her stomach started to growl.

She waited for Jimmy to hand her a share. Instead, he gave her the whole bar and said it was all hers. Like the child she really was, and forgetting her manners, she snatched it from him and quickly tore through the shiny purple and gold wrapper. Snapping off a chunky cube of ecstatic joy, she closed her eyes and started to drown in its melting sweetness.

"Blimey," Jimmy laughed out loud, "you really do like your chocolate, Jen. I'll have to remember that. Yeh, I will."

Jenny nodded her head, happily devouring chunk after chunk until her growling stomach was steadily satisfied.

"Listen. I've seen Alice and she wants you to know you can use kitchen and backroom any time you like and then there's a bath and a toilet up here. Yeh, this is a posh house. Toilet outside's okay, too. If I pay Alice she sometimes lets me have a bath here if I want. Otherwise, I can go to Bridgey Street. You can get a bath there and soap and a towel but have to pay a lot more than I give Alice. Still, I like it there. You can go for a swim, too. Love a swim. Me and Will have been chucked out a few times for messin' about. We have splash fights."

Jenny's angel was making her laugh again but all his talk about water and the baths made her realise that she had not been to the toilet in such a long while. Right now, she needed to go and was thankful that this 'posh' house had a bathroom. She asked to be excused and, from Jimmy's reaction, she realised that this was not something you needed to ask in his world.

He giggled. "'Course you can! Anyway, I'll leave you to it and I'll be back later with whatever Will gets you. Still got lipstick and some clothes to get so I'll go and do that now and bring that later, too. Oh, before I forget, Alice says, as soon as you can, she wants to see you. She'll be in the front room. Okay?"

Jenny nodded and, without a care in the world, Jimmy cheerfully embarked on his next mission.

Left alone, Jenny glanced round the room knowing that now she could make a start on creating her space, a clean, comfortable space. She looked at Jimmy's prizes left abandoned on the bed. She quickly went over and removed them, not wishing to contaminate them. They had already been on the bed for long enough. The sheets and the blanket could now be removed and evidence of what they represented soon discarded. Fresh sheets, fresh bedding. New start. Ironic, she knew that much, but it would be her own contamination and, convincing herself, yet again, that she would have control over it.

She would begin her mammoth task of cleaning and scrubbing and making changes shortly but first she needed the toilet and then she would go and see Alice. She had been summoned and, the sooner she had got that out of the way, then what was left of the day and night would be hers.

She left the room and made her way to the door at the top of the landing. She knew that this was where the bathroom must be since Jimmy had already told her that the room at the front was Alice's bedroom.

Tentatively, she opened the door, fully expecting a mess of dirt and smell but she was pleasantly surprised. Like her own room, the bathroom was functional and bare of unnecessary frills or comforts except it was relatively clean. A half used roll of toilet paper rested on the linoleum floor. Jenny tore off a few sheets and wiped the toilet seat. She pulled down her jeans and knickers and sat down. Relief. Relief, in more ways than one. Apart from a thick line of grime creating a high tide mark round the bath, some chipped enamel and a tide mark round the inside of the toilet, Jenny knew she could soon give all that she saw an easy fresh clean.

She was happy for this facility since it meant she could wash and wash and wash away her own private dirt, as many times as she needed to, and rid herself of each nightly episode performed on the bed. She decided that, once each night was over, she would remove the sheets before she went to sleep and then put them back each evening. Her own personal sheets for sleep and then her work sheets. This decision established further control and she was happy with it. Will had been right. She was grateful for the three cellophane packages.

Welded to the corner edge of the bath she saw a bar of pink soap, stuck fast in its congealed slime, and another on the sink. Jenny was keen to smell its fragrance. Above the sink hung an old tarnished mirror in need of a wipe. A used towel had been left in the bath and Jenny hoped that there would be others for use somewhere. Something else to ask Alice. In the meantime, after finishing on the toilet and washing her hands, she wiped them down on her jeans. At least the soap had a fragrance to it and a rather pleasing one. She was tempted to look at her reflection in the tarnished mirror but could not bring herself to do so. Ugly, hideous and vile is what she knew to expect staring back at her. At least the red lipstick, when applied, would change her appearance and the short, blonde hair, too. She would need the mirror then and, until such time, seeing herself was not necessary. Pretty? What did Jimmy really know?

Before leaving the bathroom she stepped into the bath to reach a top window. Some fresh air would blow away any lingering staleness. She would remember to shut it later. Carefully stepping out of the bath, and closing the bathroom door behind her, Jenny made her way downstairs to see Alice.

The idea of having to go into Alice's front room and be in her presence for long was not one Jenny embraced. She imagined what the room would be like; no doubt dirty, messy and smelly. Alice wanted to see her and Jenny wondered what else she could say and tell her that had not already been said? Alice had been pretty clear in what Jenny's work would involve.

The house was eerily quiet, save for a radio playing in the front room. A classical, haunting melody. Jenny listened for a minute before knocking on the door. The radio was switched off and Alice called out inviting Jenny in.

She opened the door slowly and stepped on to a plush, patterned carpet, soft and spongy as her feet made contact. She looked around her, mouth agape, as she digested all that she now saw. Apart from dusty surfaces highlighted by the winter sun struggling to shine through the net curtains, the room was quite splendid. A flowery paper decorated the walls, orange and yellow flower shapes totally clashing with the thick purple patterned carpet. Still, it did not seem to matter since the room emanated a cosy charm. A gas fire, with teak surround, created warmth and Jenny noticed that it was on at full power with its rows of tiny flames flickering in regimental unison. She realised she was still holding her mother's coat tightly round her, fully expecting the cold's icy vengeance to attack her again once leaving the bathroom.

Beginning to feel the warmth filling the room, she now let go of her hold and let the coat hang loosely. She wondered whether she should remove it but felt it rude not to ask first or at least be invited to do so.

The furniture in the room was typical of the modern trends that Jenny had seen before in Hell but, in Hell, the trend was expensive. Here, less so, but perfectly adequate all the same. Here, she felt and could sense that the furniture was loved and that was what mattered. Alice looked proud as she observed Jenny taking in the surroundings. The vinyl settee, with its buttoned back and its matching armchairs, complemented the carpet with its purple seat cushions. Velvety scatter cushions added a finishing touch. A wooden sideboard stretched the length of one of the walls, sleek and quite elegant. Alice sat, like a queen on her throne, in one of the armchairs by the fire. A small table was at her side with a radio taking pride of place on it. A coffee table, with Formica top and a shelf below it, stood in the centre of the room. Jenny had sometimes wondered why such tables were called coffee tables since other drinks were placed on them too. What if you preferred tea or milk? Were there tea tables or milk tables anywhere in the world? It did not really matter since she had very rarely been allowed coffee or tea or milk to drink. Water had always been the easiest of options given to her. It was quick, it was free and she didn't deserve anything else.

On the wall, above the fireplace, a clock hung majestically. Quite a feature. It resembled an image of the sun with its rays of wood matching the teak of the fireplace and sideboard. At its centre the clock's face told Jenny that it was still morning: eleven twenty-five. She was surprised since she expected it to be much later.

She started to relax in the knowledge that the afternoon would be all hers at least to make a start on her room. Seeing the time made her realise that she too would be needing a clock. An alarm clock. Panic started to set in a little since her list of wants was growing more and more. Basic items she had always taken for granted since, in Hell, except for food, there was everything and anything money could buy and more. Materialistic, all show, all unloved. She thought about the pink alarm clock that she would set to wake her each morning for school.

Alice must have noticed Jenny's mind drifting off somewhere and she needed to bring her back. "Well, lass," she said, "what do you think? Do you like it?"

Jenny's racing thoughts were halted as Alice's question demanded an answer, "Yes, yes, yes I do. It's, it's lovely," she stammered

"Well, take your coat off, lass, and sit down."

Beads of sweat had started to appear on Jenny's forehead and she was thankful that permission to remove her coat had been granted without her needing to ask.

As she removed the coat she noticed the heavy velvet curtains, draped opulently either side of the bay window, and all the trinkets and ornaments scattered in abundance on every available surface. A number of paintings graced the walls but one, in particular, caught Jenny's eye. It adorned the wall above the sideboard encapsulating the beauty of a woman with dark, sultry features. She was engaging and Jenny was drawn to the long, wavy hair perfectly coiffed over a shoulder of bare flesh. Again, Jenny's mind had been distracted and she was not aware that she had been staring at the painting with such intensity until Alice said, "Beautiful 'int she?"

Jenny nodded and Alice continued, "I used to look like that once, you know. Yeh, I did. Then, bloody hell, I looked in the mirror one day and this!" She gestured from head to toe and shrugged then laughed out loud. Jenny found it hard to believe that Alice could have ever been so beautiful and alluring and she just smiled, trying hard not to offend or make her doubts too obvious.

"Yeh, I did. Men queued up for me, you know. A real colleen. An Irish beauty. My dad were Irish. Drunken, good for nothin' sod. Anyway, I knew how to look and dress. I look at her and remember the times when I were workin' the streets and makin' good money. Then, I met Bert and he brought me here. I set up business for myself in this place. He didn't mind so long as I was here to look after him and keep him company and please his needs whenever he wanted me to, which weren't a lot of the time. He loved me in his way and I cared for him. Back then's when I were as pretty as that picture and then the years crept up on me and Bert died. Still miss the old man. Clever man and he liked his music too. Nice classical stuff. Passed that on to me. Nothing nicer than listenin' to some Beethoven or Chopin. No bloody television here. Can't stand 'em. Radio's my friend.

"Anyways, Bert paid the rent but, when he'd gone, it were all down to me. So, I got one of the girls off street, and there's enough of 'em to come here and do

70

business, as well as myself. Yeh, always had a good thing goin'. Fella as owns these houses is a right bloody crook and, so long as I pay him that bit more in rent, he turns a blind eye to what goes on. Neighbours are all nice and, anyhow, none of 'em dares say anythin' 'cause that bloody crook'd get 'em chucked out and have men round to give 'em a beatin'. They none of 'em can afford trouble and so best to keep their mouths shut. A man with some power. Greedy bastard. He makes a good extra from this place. He does that. Still, I'm lucky. Had lots of girls come and go over the years and I got lazy. Always tried to keep a nice and clean place but, since fat has decided to like me and cling on for dear life, it's harder for me to do things. The girls that have been here, over time, I tell anyone, as wants to know, that they are live-in hired help. That way, it covers what really goes on."

Jenny was intrigued and began to relax a little. Leaning back on the buttoned vinyl of the settee, she waited for Alice to continue. The sour, acrid invasion of Alice's feet now started to become awkwardly discernible and Jenny wondered had the invasion been there from her first entering the room or had she been too preoccupied to notice?

As if reading her thoughts, or it could have been the slight twitching of Jenny's nose, Alice blurted out, "Jen, Jenny. Do I smell?"

Jenny was shocked. Mortified. What could she say?

"Hey, lass. Don't be shy. Say it as it is. I know I do and it's bloody awful. Emma's leavin' has left me right in the shit. More ways than one and not just 'cause I've got to get Shirl in and she's a bloody pain. Miserable beggar she is. Always moanin'. Anyway, she's proper glad to get back out there. She knows, though, she'll be doin' tonight and tomorrow and can use my room and then that's it. She'll still be comin' to do a couple of nights when you take some time off but weekends, in the future, you'll always be doin'. Don't worry, she'll never use your room. She'll be usin' mine, like I said. You'll never see her. She's not interested in anyone but herself and, anyways, she knows I'll give her a bit extra for doin' your days off and, if she can't, there's always someone else as will. Emma used to like takin' Mondays and Tuesdays off. You can take same if you want.

"Anyways, we'll see. I still do a few myself but not full job anymore. Have my regulars that call me on that there phone over there. They let me know they're on their way and I'll meet 'em in the back privy for a good old hand job. Do you know, for some bloody reason, men like these crummy, dark places. Don't bother me. It's easy money.

"Sometimes they don't ring and just turn up knockin' on the back window. Door's always open and most of 'em as comes don't want to get noticed so are always careful as to their comings and goings. Our regulars tend to be friends of friends that come here, or have been here, and so know to ring or just come round the back. Number's in the telephone book under Grundy. I know we weren't married but I've always taken Bert's name. Anyways, business never really stops, Jen. It's mainly our regulars and most of 'em are easy and some don't even do much. They'll just want to look at you and do it to 'emselves. Sad sods. You'll soon get used to their ways."

Jenny tried to comprehend the extent of Alice's matter of fact approach but was not disturbed by what she had heard. She had experienced degradation too often to be bothered now.

The room's haphazard yet intriguing mix of colours and the restful warmth of the flickering flames, as they continued their uniform dance behind the fire's iron grille, made Jenny want to sink and slide further down against the buttoned vinyl back of the settee. What she felt was unusually surreal. She felt safe and comfortable.

Alice opened the top drawer of the cabinet, on the other side of her chair, without having to move. Everything within easy reach. She took out a small box

"Take it you know what these are?" she said.

Jenny was not sure since she had never seen a box like it before. She sat up straight as she took a closer look.

"These are Durex or Johnnies, as we call 'em."

Jenny flinched at the mention of a name from Hell. Johnny, John. The padlock on the door of her mental cupboard rattled until Alice started to explain and it became firmly fixed once more

"Yeh, we call 'em Johnnies. Told it comes from the name John Thomas which is slang for penis. Don't know why 'cause I've not a bloody clue who John Thomas were or what he's gotta do with a ruddy penis. Well, there you go. Anyways, they're even called rubbers 'cause they're made out of rubber. Well, Jen, thing is, you make bloody well sure that, if any of 'em, want full sex they'd better put one of these on. Some have their own but, if they don't, you can give 'em one of these. Don't want you gettin' any trouble down there, do you know what I mean? You've already said you don't have your monthlies so gettin' in the club won't happen but these'll keep you clean. Do you know what I mean?"

Alice had said it again, 'do you know what I mean?' and Jenny was clueless. She knew what the Johnnies, what the rubbers were but had never known a name for them. Now she did but what was 'the club'? She thought it best just to nod her head and accept all that Alice was telling her. For now, it would be easier.

"Well, now we've got that out of the way, here you are." She handed over the box and smiled.

"Right. Now, as I were telling you before about Emma, yeh?"

So much had been said since then and Jenny could not quite think what else Alice had to tell her. Still, she nodded.

"Well," Alice continued, "over the years me and my girls have always had an arrangement. They earn a bit extra for lookin' after me too and keepin' on top of things in the house like cleanin' and tidyin' and makin' sure bin's left out for the bin men that come on a Thursday. All rooms'll need doin'. In here's easy. Not long been decorated by a fella I know and some new furniture. New carpets and curtains too. It's lovely, don't you think?

"There's a ewbank in the cupboard under the stairs and some other stuff for doin' the cleanin' and that. In here just needs dustin' sometimes and I try to do it myself as much as I can. It's easier for me, too, usin' the ewbank rather than the hoover. It weighs a bloody ton does that bloody hoover and the wire keeps gettin' caught round things. Someone young like yourself, though, could manage the hoover. Even though there's not a scrap on you, somethin' tells me you're a lot stronger than you look. Jimmy's told me you want to clean your own room and do it up. Listen, sounds to me as you're a good lass. Now, are you okay to clean for me?"

Alice paused and Jenny could only nod again, this time pleased at the task in hand. She would enjoy making the rest of the house more habitable and it would mean she could use the kitchen and the back room whenever she wanted to. It was obvious that the overflowing bin in the yard had not been put out for emptying since Emma had left. Jenny would do something about the overflowing contents, that she recalled from the night before, and its putrid pile. She could envisage the smell eventually seeping its way through the brickwork and window gaps and penetrating the very fabric of her room. No. No, she had to address that and soon.

Her mind was racing again. Alice halted her thoughts. "Also, Jen," she said, "it means me as well."

Jenny could not quite grasp what Alice was now saying and, for the first time, she spoke. Up until now she had only nodded and listened attentively.

"Sorry, Alice," she uttered, nervously, "I don't quite understand what you mean."

The formidable, frightening figure of the previous night now looked fragile and Jenny felt sad as she sensed Alice's embarrassment.

"It's like this, Jen. I've got so bloody big I don't find it easy anymore to do things for myself like gettin' in the bath on my own and then gettin' out and dryin' myself. I can't even bend over to wipe my feet if I manage to get to soak 'em in a bowl. I can just about manage to get myself up the stairs. It takes a lot longer now than it did when I could bloody well fly up! Anyways, now and again, I might just sleep in here and put my feet up on that there pouffe. Try not to make habit of it though.

"Hey, Jen. I'd love a bath. I know I stink. You'll get paid extra on top of your earnings. Told you that already. You're a bit younger than some of the other lasses that's been here but, again, somethin' tells me you'll do a much better job of everythin'."

Jenny was shocked. She had never had to bath anyone before nor had she ever seen a naked woman before, not even the bitch in Hell. How bad could it be to see Alice in all her glory? She felt she wanted to help. She felt she needed to help. After all, in her own way, Alice was helping her and giving her so much freedom, apart from the night time work. Still, in life, even at just fourteen years old, Jenny knew that actions had consequences and, if all this now was the consequence of the action that she had been driven to take, then she was thankful.

Alice was staring at her hopefully and Jenny nodded her head, "Yes, Alice. That's fine. I'll try my very best."

Alice's flabby face, her thin lips now just slightly stained with the gaudy, orange emblem of her trade, beamed.

"Oh, Jen, love. Thanks. I know you'll try your best. Yeh, I know you will. You're a good girl. Well, maybe soon you'll give me a bloody good scrub then that cute, little nose'll stop twitchin'. Don't think I've not noticed," and she burst out laughing.

Jenny had not realised her distaste had been so obvious and she was horrified. All she felt she could do now was laugh since Alice's mirth seemed to be inviting her to do so.

"Well, now that's out the way, Jimmy says you're wantin' to ask me a few things. Well, go on. I'm all ears, dirty ones mind," and she started laughing again. Her merriment brought with it a succession of wind pumps. The beautiful lady that she had never forgotten, wearing the red lipstick, would call them bottom burps when admonishing someone in the classroom for delivering them with glee and much too often. A memory that actually made Jenny smile back then when she had nothing to smile about. Now, Jenny was smiling again as each pop, pop made Alice laugh all the more until eventually she calmed down. Simulating a measure of seriousness, Alice's lips tried hard not to spread wide and burst forth into laughter again.

From first entering the room Jenny had completely forgotten that she was going to ask Alice about a few things.

"Okay Jen, love. What was it you were wantin' to ask?"

"Oh, yes," she said. "Of course. Erm. Well, Alice, I would like to cut my hair and maybe dye it blonde like yours and I wondered what to use and where I could find scissors, if you happen to have a pair in the house?"

She paused before continuing, "I've already used the bathroom and wondered where I might be able to find clean towels?"

Jenny wanted to ask about a lamp for her room but thought maybe she had asked for too much already.

Then, she decided well, in for a penny… "Oh, and I was also wondering whether I might be able to find a spare lamp for my room or a lamp shade, if not, for the ceiling light? If neither then it doesn't matter. Once I start earning money of my own I can always go out and buy them."

Alice was still smiling and she nodded. "Aye Jen, love. There's all sorts in this house. Hardly throw anythin' out. In the cupboard under the stairs you'll find lots of different things. Everythin's in that cupboard. There should be an old lamp in there with a bulb still in it. Used to be in here before I got new. Yeh, go and have a good rummage. Take what you like."

"Thank you very much, Alice."

"My, you're a posh one. Good manners, well spoken. Hey, and your hair is lovely, by the way. Don't know why you want to change it."

Jenny had never thought of her hair as being lovely before. Long and dark and lank, dull and non-descript, just like herself. Anyway, she needed to disguise her appearance. She had to. Jenny Smith would be blonde.

"Listen, I know you're a runaway," Alice continued, "and there'll be a reason why you did. I'll never ask you why. You'll let me know when and if you wants me to know. I were a runaway myself but I'll tell you about that some other time. Now, is there somethin' else you'll be wantin'?"

"Yes, there is if you don't mind? Would you happen to have a spare alarm clock?"

"Alarm clock? Alarm clock?" Alice repeated to herself, as if trying to remember something, then she smiled. In fact, it suddenly dawned on Jenny that Alice had not stopped smiling from the moment Jenny had first come into the room.

"Yeh, Jen. Get up and look in the top middle drawer of that there sideboard. Think there's one in there that's never been used."

Jenny went over and opened the drawer. The top drawer had three compartments – a wide space in the middle and a narrower one on either side. The drawer was tidy, its contents untouched. Jenny saw a neat pile of papers in the middle and, on the right hand side, a small, square, brown leather box

"Well? Is it there?" Alice asked.

Jenny was not sure and lifted up the box.

"Yeh, that's it. They call 'em travel clocks. Not that I've travelled anywhere and never will do. One of Jimmy's presents! He'll pick up anythin'. Still, it's come in useful now. Open it and it should still be ok. Easy to use. You're a smart girl. Should be able to sort it."

Jenny opened the small clasp on the front. Inside was a clock. Its face could rest on the base and from the side it resembled a triangle. Jenny thought it was neat and still so new. She could not wait to adjust it. She looked at the sun clock on the wall, big and bold and proud displaying its time and, in her hand, its dainty counterpart that could do the same. No difference. Just show.

On its bright dial the sun clock exhibited twelve twenty-four and Jenny was amazed at just how long she had been in Alice's company. She felt at ease and comfortable, feelings that were quite unfamiliar to her and she liked them. She picked up her coat, and was about to say thank you once more, when Alice asked, "Aren't you forgettin' somethin'?"

Jenny was somewhat confused. "Pardon?"

"Scissors? Hair stuff? Towels?"

"Oh, of course. Sorry," she said, relieved, thinking she may have done something to upset Alice. She was so accustomed to being accused and blamed for even breathing and so, constantly, on the alert. Such was Hell. She was not used to peace and calm and now she really, really smiled at Alice. Alice smiled back and, for the first time, Jenny saw some of the beauty resembling the lady in the painting.

She wanted to show her appreciation and, before Alice could say any more, Jenny asked, "Alice? Later, would you like me to get the bath ready and I'll help you up the stairs and we'll take it from there?"

Alice's face positively shone with delight. "Oh, Jen, love. Yeh, yeh I would. Sooner the better then we can get rid of this stink and I'll come out smellin' of roses.

Yeh, smellin' of roses. Aye, literally. Got this lovely bubble bath stuff off market and it smells of roses. It's gorgeous. You'll find it in the immersion cupboard the other end of the bath. There's some Radox there as well. I like a sprinklin' of that too. Aye, why not? That's what I say. Why not? You'll find clean towels in that there immersion cupboard too and a couple of boxes of my hair dye. Maybe you could do my hair as well? I'll show you what to do and then you could do yours too. Do you think?"

"Yeh. I think," said Jenny, nodding and knowing full well that her take on Alice's way of speaking would certainly not cause offence.

She was right. Alice laughed out loud, "Go on, you cheeky little bugger! Get out and go and get yourself sorted. Oh, by the way, you'll find scissors in the kitchen. Take a pair. Take a couple. You can keep 'em. I've got a few. Now, get gone!"

With that, Jenny left the room shutting the door gently behind her. Within seconds a classical, melodious tune was guiding her back up the stairs.

CHAPTER 5

'The secret of change is to focus all of your energy, not
on fighting the old, but on building the new.'

Socrates

Making Changes

Sunlight had replaced the previous night's squall. Its
white beams, despite the open curtains, still struggled to
sneak through the smudged blurs of dirt so decisively
fixed to the single pane of glass. Inside and out.

What light managed to infiltrate simply served to
illuminate the room's grubbiness. At best, the inside of
the window could be wiped clean; the outside would
continue to be ruled by the elements. Still, it was
something.

The drab, grey curtains were crying out to be yanked
down and replaced. The sooner the better. They had
long since outgrown their friendship with the window

and it was time for something new, well, as new as could be achieved with just scissors and nappy pins. The material, though, was very pretty and Jenny knew it would make such a difference.

Itching to make a start on all she wanted to do, she first needed to find the scissors in the kitchen and the sweeping brush and mop and bucket that Jimmy had left for her there. Time then to move on and explore 'the cupboard under the stairs'! A mystery that, for some reason, Jenny felt intrigued by and Alice's references to it had made her smile.

She was smiling now and it dawned on her that, yet again, she had been smiling such a lot, ever since Jimmy's laughter and giggling had roused her from deep sleep earlier that day. She remembered reading something once, about Mother Teresa, who had said: 'Peace begins with a smile'. She had never before understood the full extent of these words since she had little, if any, affinity with the concept of peace. Now, in a funny sort of way, she did understand.

Time spent with Jimmy and Alice had been quite bizarre, a mix of emotions, unfamiliar yet pleasing. Emotions, a number of which, inevitably made her want to smile. Despite the lives they led, smiles and laughter were in abundance. Simple joy and it made her feel safe. Maybe time with them was beginning to make her see a tiny fragment of the rainbow blotches in the sky; the ones she would find herself searching for in dreams.

Jenny had already resigned herself to the fact that soon she would play a part in this other life that Jimmy and Alice both led; the night time episodes where her young body would be used, like a machine, to make money. Her resolve was such that she knew she could distance and detach her mind from each encounter; all her feelings lifted and spirited away to another dimension.

For now, looking around the room, she felt a steadiness, as if all the storms that had been raging within her for so long were, instead, a mild whispering breeze. Her brain felt free to create something of her own without being frightened or answerable to anyone. A metamorphosis that mattered. It would hold her to this new life that she felt was meant to be experienced, as she walked along the road to her cotton candy dream.

With a spring in her step, she left the room and made her way downstairs to the kitchen and the 'cupboard under the stairs'.

Jenny's recollection of the kitchen, from the previous evening, had not been favourable and she was relieved to find that some attempt had at least been made with the washing up. The sink still held grease around its rim and the backsplash was splattered with stains. A frying pan sat abandoned on the stove, the grease fat now set solid and wax like. The smell of frying still lingered and

Jenny knew that Alice must have had her fill of breakfast earlier that morning.

Despite the cold outside and the putrid contents of the overflowing bin in the backyard, Jenny opened the window a fraction. A blast of air would help eliminate the cloying, rancid aroma of grease fat. She would remember to shut it before going back upstairs. The overflowing bin she would tackle another time. Once the bin men had emptied its mix of rubbish she would establish control. She would make sure to put the bin out for them on Thursday recalling Alice previously telling her that, that was when they came.

A couple of small kitchen units stood side by side and a cabinet, the like of which Jenny had never seen before, held pride of place, standing tall, and squeezed in next to them. In Hell the kitchen had been ultra modern and streamlined and state of the art. All sham. All show. Rarely used for its true purpose.

She opened the top drawers of the units and found an array of utensils and, in one of the drawers, some scissors. A few pairs, in fact. Alice had said she could take what she wanted and so Jenny chose a large pair, that would be ideal for cutting material, and a smaller pair for when she would cut her hair. Jimmy had left the sweeping brush leaning up against the wall by the back door where she had also found the mop and bucket.

Still wearing her mother's coat, she put the scissors inside its deep pockets and, picking up the sweeping brush in one hand, and the mop and bucket in the other, she turned her back on the kitchen.

Years of forced domesticity had given her experience enough to know that the kitchen could easily be restored to some order and sparkle and shine. Not an unpleasant chore at all, unlike a lot of the messes she had been used to dealing with for as long as she could remember. The vomit, the wee and sometimes the faeces soaked and caught up in the cream coloured luxury shag pile much favoured in that prison. She knew exactly where all the stains were. Even when brand new carpets were fitted the colour was the same creamy white shag pile except the pile was thicker, longer and plusher. Even harder to clean any accidents up from its trappings. The bitch did not have a clue, nor ever remembered her knickers having to be changed or being guided to bed. Jenny knew and feared that, if messes were left, she would be accused and blamed for the fouling and unmentionable vestiges that only an alcoholic could leave behind. With blame came hurt and so she had always done her best to avoid it. Yes, she was used to cleaning up mess. Alice's kitchen would be easy.

Reprimanding herself for once more allowing the padlock on her mental cupboard to loosen and unfix itself, and the box, set far back in its darkest depths, to reveal some of its contents, Jenny quickly locked it again and turned her attention to another cupboard; a cupboard that she wanted to open. A tangible cupboard that promised treasure of sorts and one that was waiting for her to explore.

Jenny was not disappointed. 'The cupboard under the stairs' was indeed a veritable Aladdin's cave and she could not have been more thrilled.

On first opening the door, she had felt for a light switch and was grateful when she found one. The light shed some answers to what was stored in this den. A mish-mash of contents. A number of shelves housed a selection of cleaning materials: Vim, Ajax, Brillo pads, Fairy Liquid, Tide, everything she needed and more. Tide? There must have been a washing machine in the kitchen that she had not noticed. She would look later and also put the cleaning products, Jimmy had brought her, on the cupboard shelves alongside the others too.

Alice's ewbank stood at the front of the cupboard begging to be used. First in line. The hoover, with its flexed wire carelessly left in a tangle, had been left abandoned close by. A number of cardboard boxes, varying in size, were set back in the cupboard and, bringing out the ewbank and hoover, Jenny bent down to retrieve a couple of them. As she started to slide forward the first box, hiding behind it, she discovered a small electric heater, plug intact. Joy of joys! What a find! Its two bars of electric warmth would take off the damp and chill in her room and she could not wait to plug in the magic. Despite the marks and scars of age on its cream and gold surround, Jenny loved it.

Her joy grew when she next found the table lamp that Alice had said would probably be there. It was in the first box, along with other discarded bric-a-brac. With care she gently lifted it out, its fringed floral shade still cheerfully in place. Together with bulb and plug, it was ready to cast a warm, cosy glow once more. She somehow knew that these two much needed finds would not let her down. Fingers crossed.

Jenny had all that she needed for the time being but curiosity drew her to the second box that she had struggled to slide out. Whatever was housed inside was heavy and, before having to push her weight against it to nudge it back, she took a peek. What she found, stacked in rows, one on top of the other, took her breath away.

Books! All the same size. Such heavy, magnificent tomes. This was true treasure. As if handling a delicate flower, Jenny lifted one up. Her hand moved instinctively over the book, her fingers tracing the binding and gold lettering and appreciating its grainy red leather bound beauty.

One by one, she continued to lift out the rest. A whole set of Encyclopedia Britannica. They were in no particular order but had been stacked carefully and not just thrown in. An avalanche of knowledge. She had only ever seen encyclopedias in the library at school. To have one's own personal set was something she could never have envisaged. Not in a million years.

 Reading had always been a mainstay in her life. She had been a fervid member of the school library and remembered the library monitor duties she had been awarded with at her primary school. She was never given money to spend until she was older and had started at her senior school when money was given at Birthdays and Christmases. More often than not, she would put by what little money was given to her and add it to the bus fares she saved, whenever she could manage to leave the house extra early, and walk to school instead. Attending the local grammar school had meant she was old enough to get a bus to school instead of being chauffeured by a very kind and knowledgeable man she had learned so much from.

Her visits to the local second hand shop in the village were definitely worth the sacrifice of not being transported by bus to school. She had her pick of tatty paperbacks with curled up corners, hard backs-some with their once glossy jackets missing, science fiction, crime novels, romance, assorted travel books and so much more. A bargain haven where she had acquired a selection of staunch companions whose trials and tribulations, wonder and cheer, and whose 'happy ever afters', penned by masters of the written word, she was able to share. Fiction, but now she had a whole set of non-fiction, to hand, and was more than satisfied since a world without reading meant she had absolutely nothing.

So much had occurred, since leaving the fires of Hell, that she had not had a chance to even think about what she loved most in the world. The only thing. She had escaped and had left all her papery pages behind; pages she knew could often soothe her anxieties and constant fears, restoring a measure of mental calmness when all around her was turmoil.

There were ten volumes in total and a dictionary. Each volume was classed in alphabetical order, each page waiting to speak and impart knowledge, fountains of knowledge. Dear, reliable allies that she knew would bring the pleasure of discovery in her quest for learning. Her teachers had always told her she was bright and, despite her regular absences, ever since the devil had come home to stay, Jenny knew that, sometimes, they found it hard to keep up with her. A 'delicate child', she was classified as being, which accounted for why she missed so much school. If only they had known. If only they had known the truth.

Jenny had her own school now in ten volumes and a dictionary, a true bible of learning and vocabulary. She knew that she could look up one thing and accidentally encounter something even more interesting and remote on an adjacent page and she could not wait.

She put the volumes carefully back inside the box before returning them to the cupboard. Even though Alice had told her to, 'have a good rummage' and to, 'take what you like', Jenny felt it was only right to ask first.

Before closing the cupboard door, she picked up a plastic bucket, some cloths and took the Vim from one of the shelves. Jenny was glad to have found it there. She had used it before and knew it to be the salvation of all grimy tide marks round baths, sinks and toilets. Yes, it would prove very useful. She would need to come back downstairs a few times to collect all the other items. First, though, she would take the sweeping brush and mop and bucket but not before shutting the window in the kitchen.

After stripping the bed, yanking down the tired curtains and leaving them all in a heap on the landing outside, Jenny removed her mother's coat and draped it over the bannister. Before anything else she went to shut the window in the bathroom so that it would not be too cold for Alice later.

Her room was now a complete blank canvas and, like an artist, her mind all the while directing her hand, she started to compose her masterpiece.

Some two hours later, she was not quite sure, but with the travel alarm clock, now sitting on the dresser giving Jenny an indication, she stepped back to behold the result of her undertaking. An undertaking that, although not quite the finished masterpiece she had wanted, was still pleasing.

Apart from the ceiling, every possible surface had been swept and cleaned. Even the walls. As she had carefully stood on the wooden chair wiping them down with her mix of liquid and bleach, they didn't appear half as grubby.

The window shone on the inside. No streaks; its grainy, stained exterior envious. Over the years she had learned that to wet a window with a cloth first and then wipe dry immediately with tissue paper usually did the trick. When she could, she would buy toilet tissue to replace what she had used for this purpose.

The curtains had been an easy addition. Jenny's keen eye for detail had allowed her to cut two relatively straight pieces of the material and then another two. The material was such that it did not fray all that much and she just snipped away at any random threads. Standing on the wooden chair, doubling up the material, she folded the tops over the rail and, with the nappy pins, she secured the tops across. She continued to do the same on the other side. Such a creation. So simple yet serviceable. Although, when she shut them and opened them again the movement across wasn't smooth it was still an achievement and would more than do. If she could find nails and a hammer she would not need to open them; she could just tie them back. She had more than enough material left to cut out ribbon ties and the ties could then be held on to the nails. She would ask Alice for nails and hammer and she smiled. Something told her that she would be directed once more to the 'cupboard under the stairs'.

As she continued to look around her, Jenny's smile broadened. Her spirits had been further lifted when earlier she had plugged in the electric fire and the lamp. They both still worked. The fire's two bars of orange glow had now crept into the corners of the room, radiating a semblance of warmth and, together with the lamp casting a restful charm of its own, Jenny no longer felt suffocated. Leaving the fire switched on to continue its much appreciated job, Jenny unplugged the table lamp since it was not yet needed. She looked forward to switching it back on later.

It was uplifting to see such a part-finished canvas any artist would be proud of. When she had time she would take a closer look at all the bric-a-brac she had seen in the box, where the lamp had been lying prettily on top, and see what she could find by way of a choice ornament or two. Jenny was in no doubt that she would unearth something and was already looking forward. The room needed a few finishing touches.

One thing she still had left to do was to make the bed but not until she had let the mattress air for a while longer.

Jimmy had not yet returned with the rest of the things he had set out to get her. She knew he would and, until such time, she would go and do what needed to be done in the bathroom and then run a bath for Alice.

CHAPTER 6

'Over and over again, I have experienced the quieting
influence of rose scent on a disturbed state of mind.'

Louise Beebe Wilder, 1878-1938

Bonding

The water was hot and the sound of it pouring, without
a care, into the bath, was comforting. As the bubbles
formed and foamed and mingled with the added bonus
of Radox crystals, the ones Alice had mentioned earlier,
an infusion of scents became trapped in the steam that
now filled the bathroom space.

Jenny sat down on the toilet seat and closed her eyes,
savouring the sweet flowery perfume and the discernible
essence of roses, delicate and fine. A very gentle and
kind man once told her that a rose is truly a thing of
beauty and each different colour has a special meaning.
His favourite colour rose was deep pink, an expression
of thanks and gratitude when given to someone. At that

moment the deep pink scented liquid, creating its peaks of foamy bubbles, could not have been more fitting. The bathroom door was wide open, as well as the door to her own room and Alice's, so that the timeless, intoxicating fragrance could float further away and gently touch the rest of the house. A worthy thought and one which Jenny found soothing. The scent was quite beautiful.

Looking around her now Jenny was pleased. It had not taken her long to do what was needed in the bathroom. The Vim and the bleach, and a touch of washing up liquid, had made light work of this chore. She had enjoyed bringing a shine back to the enamelled surfaces and getting rid of the stickiness that had gripped itself to the linoleum floor. Although she had not noticed earlier, when she had first opened the window and then gone back later to close it again, the heavy net curtain that was there looked quite new and provided the privacy much sought after in a room such as this. The cupboard, at the end of the bath, just like the 'cupboard under the stairs', proved yet another store of treasure!

On first opening it, Jenny's eyes lit up. As well as an abundance of towels, randomly folded, one on top of the other in two piles, different colours and sizes, the cupboard housed an array of bathroom products. On one of the shelves Jenny found two bottles of Alice's much favoured rose bubble bath and a box of Radox along with talcum powder, soaps, hairspray, Astral face cream, a few bottles of shampoo and, of course, hair bleaching dye. Not just one box but enough to last a lifetime! Slight exaggeration but Alice had clearly made sure she was not going to run out any time soon. The instructions on the back of the box were self-explanatory but, no doubt, Alice would confirm what exactly was required to achieve the desired 'Born Blonde' look that held claim to this magic product. A look Jenny was now eager to apply along with cutting her hair. Until such time, she would refrain from looking in the mirror. She had not long given the glass a wipe down and it now hung on the wall waiting to acknowledge its next reflection.

The cupboard had been warm inside. The immersion tank, clearly having been switched on for quite some time and now full of hot water emptying freely into the bath, made it an ideal space to keep towels warm and ready to wrap around dripping nakedness, like a hug. Clearly, Alice could afford such a luxury. Jenny, however, knew only too well that switching on the immersion heater was expensive and she would never take advantage. She was used to having to wash in cold water. She was never allowed to switch on the hot water and the bitch in Hell would very often forget to do so. Neither was she ever allowed to take a shower. Instant hot water. Another addition to the sham and show of Hell. An addition only ever afforded to the bitch and Him and sometimes even taken together.

Her one and only time in the shower had been in the very early hours of Friday morning (a quick mathematical reckoning in her brain told her some thirty-eight hours ago, give or take). Yes, her one and only time in the forbidden shower. She had stood in there for what seemed hours, as the hot water cascaded over her body and washed away evidence of her vileness. They had made her feel vile. They were vile and now their vileness, their 'bloody' vileness was being washed away. Jenny had watched its redness turn to pink and stain the white of the bath and the white surround tiles. She had eventually turned off the shower, stepped out of the bath leaving the stained mess behind. No need to clean it now. No need to clean that horrid mausoleum ever again.

The bubbles now rising and starting to form peaks over the bath brought Jenny back from yet another black thought that was meant to be locked away. How many times, how many more times would these thoughts escape? She decided right then that maybe she just had to come to terms with the fact that her mental cupboard was not quite ready yet to be made fully secure, considering how many reprimands she had given herself so far that day.

She stood up and turned off the taps. The bath looked so inviting and, by the time she had helped Alice up the stairs, the temperature would be just right. High up on the main wall of the bathroom was an electric heater whose string pull Jenny had located outside the door. A welcome addition and one whose string Jenny rendered into action before going downstairs. A cocoon of bubbled bliss awaited their return.

Alice's absolute delight, even as she struggled up the stairs with Jenny close at hand, was endearing. All the while uttering, "Thanks, Jen. Eee, thanks Jen, luv."

Jenny was assured that Alice could manage the stairs quite well on her own, albeit slowly. However, she knew that stepping in and out of the bath and drying herself properly was another matter. Alice had told her this much already and now, with Jenny to help her, Alice could not wait to be totally immersed. Catching her breath on the landing, she looked at Jenny and smiled, "Well, Jen, luv," she said, "you know what they say, don't you?"

Jenny shook her head.

"They say, we can't usually smell ourselves but, when we can, then we must stink to high heaven and I bloody well stink. So, come on, I can smell the roses from here. Aye, I can, lass."

The bathroom was everything Jenny had wanted it to be for Alice and she knew Alice was more than pleased.

"Bloody hell," Alice muttered slowly, "bloody hell," and, with that, she quickly undid the buttons on her dress and let it slide to the floor. Jenny was taken completely unawares and, for a second, just stared. Naked, except for knickers that just about fit her frame, Alice, unabashed, stood there in all her splendid glory. Her large breasts hung freely and all her fleshy curves and folds rolled seamlessly into each other, all pink and unblemished. Jenny thought of her own body. The complete opposite. Scraggy, skinny, bruised and marked.

"Well? What do you think?" Alice giggled, with hand on hip in a pose, "Bloody gorgeous, yeh?"

Jenny blushed, aware that Alice had caught her staring. She smiled and could not help but giggle too.

"Come on. Let's get me in," she said, removing her knickers.

Jenny tried hard not to breathe in, not wanting to smell Alice's stale sweat and the strong odour from between the legs that had not had the exclusivity of soap and water for some time.

She had never had to help anyone get into a bath before and she was not exactly sure what to do. Whenever the bitch in Hell had needed to be cleaned up it was a matter of a wash down with soap and a flannel and not getting her into a bath.

Her thoughts drifting once more, Jenny need not have worried since Alice had already started the process unaided. She managed to bend forward and lean onto the window sill slowly lifting one leg over the bath and then the other, all the while her weight supported by the sill. Jenny suspected that maybe, at some time or another, Alice had probably slipped or fallen getting in or out of the bath and it had unnerved her so now, having someone there just in case, gave her much needed reassurance. Jenny knew that, despite her own diminutive frame, panic and fear could release a strength, a ridiculous strength to weight ratio that she had exercised already and so, should anything happen now, she knew she would be able to deal with it.

Supporting Alice under one elbow, Jenny helped to ease her slowly and carefully into the water. With a huge sigh of relief, Alice surrendered herself to the rose petal bubbles, closing her eyes and relaxing in weightless abandon. Alice was happy.

Jenny sat down on the toilet seat and watched her. It was quiet, peaceful and warm and, after all the day's events, she suddenly felt overwhelmingly tired. Outside, the light of day was beginning to fade giving way to the early, velvety dark of a winter's evening. Jenny thought of switching on the light but did not want to disturb the restful ambience. Still, she knew she would have to eventually but not just yet. She wondered what the time was and thought of Jimmy. She had expected him to be back by now. She stood up and broke the silence for a moment.

"Alice, I shan't be a minute."

She had decided to go to her room and find out exactly what time it was.

Alice opened her eyes. "Okay, Jen, luv. No worries. I'm in Heaven, luv. I am that."

Jenny opened the door, leaving it slightly ajar, as she went to her room. She was glad she had kept the electric fire on, as its two bars of golden glow had now conquered the frigid cold that had held its command in this room for far too long. The cold had competition and, if Jenny was allowed to use the electricity when required, then she knew that the cold would no longer be a threat. Something told her that, so long as she was earning her keep, then Alice would let her use whatever she wanted.

The travel alarm clock told her it was still only 4.23pm and not as late as Jenny had first thought. She was pleased. It gave her time to manage some of the things she wanted to do before completely isolating herself from what she knew would be taking place elsewhere in the house that evening. She had the bed to make and she wanted to ask Alice about a hammer and nails and the encyclopedias. Already she had an idea on how to arrange and display the set of wondrous knowledge in her room and looked forward to it. But, first things first, Alice's bath and there was still plenty of time to try and restore Alice's 'Born Blonde 'look if she wanted her to.

Alice was sitting up in the bath and, flannel and soap in hand, was busy scrubbing herself quite merrily when Jenny got back.

"Here you are Jen, luv," she said, holding up the flannel and soap, "do me a favour and give my feet a good scrub. A bloody good scrub."

Jenny happily obliged. Alice started to giggle and laugh with each tickling but glorious application of rough flannel and, once again, she had Jenny giggling and laughing too. Such a strange but bonding moment and

Jenny felt endeared even more to this bubbly, cheery woman.

"Alice? Would you like me to do your hair?"

"I tell you what, Jen. I take it you found the stuff? Well, what we'll do is put the first part on now and then, 'cause mine's already blonde and only needs touchin' up, once you've mixed all as it tells you on the box and put it on, we can leave it for around twenty minutes. Don't have to wet my hair for that bit. After that we can wash it out. If you look in the cupboard you'll find a hand shower. It's pink. Bath's still warm so you can leave me here and then, in twenty minutes, put the hand shower on the bath taps there and we're done. Easy, then we're good to go and I can get out of here and you can help me get dry and ready. There's clean knickers in my bedroom, top drawer, and then we'll pick out a clean dress. Do you know? I've got new slippers. I think I'll wear those too. They're in the wardrobe. And, we can throw them smelly things out."

Alice pointed to the discarded vehicles of sweat by the bath. The heavy scent of roses had disguised the horrid smell and Jenny was thankful, except she knew she would be the one having to remove them. Still, she did not mind at all. She had dealt with far worse.

"Alright, Jen. Let's make a start," and, with that, Jenny brought the box out, read the instructions and proceeded in her task, carefully prompted by Alice.

Before long Alice was all dried and ready, wearing clean knickers and dress and brand new slippers. Smelling fresh and talcum powdery she said she felt like a million dollars.

"Right, let's get downstairs and have ourselves a cup o' tea."

Jenny nodded and, as Alice started to make her way downstairs unassisted, Jenny excused herself for a second and quickly went back into the bathroom.

A sprinkling of Vim, and a quick wipe down with the used towels, soon got rid of the scum and tide mark left from Alice's time spent in the scented bubbles. Scooping up the towels and Alice's dirty clothing, Jenny put them in the laundry box she had found just outside the bathroom.

Before going down to join Alice, she went back to her room to unplug the electric heater. It had done its job for the time being and Jenny was content. As she made to leave the room she heard voices and, next thing she knew, Jimmy was hurtling his way up the stairs.

"Jen? Jen? It's me!"

He came bounding into the room and Jenny decided to switch on the lamp. It was now beginning to get dark and the lamplight would be needed to receive whatever Jimmy had managed to bring her.

Jimmy looked around him and delivered a long, low whistle of approval.

"Blimey, Jen," he said. "You've been busy. Nice. Yeh, this is nice. Really nice. Gosh. Smells nice up here too. Bet you're happy. You should be. You've done good. Bloody good. Anyways, got you these. Will got you a couple of blankets, like he said, and then there's lipstick. Red like you said. Got some knickers. Alice said to get you some and I picked a few pairs up from a place in the Market Hall. Got you a frock from there too.

"It's a grand place is the Hall. It's like the market but it's all inside and it's massive! I saw these frocks all hangin' up high around this stall and then there were some on a rail too. Thought of you when I saw this frock. It's pretty and it's got reds and pinks in it and it'll go with that red lipstick. I'll leave everythin' here on the bed and you can sort it after you've had your tea."

"My tea?" Jenny asked

"Yeh. That's why I'm a bit late back. I were waitin' for the chippy to open. I got you and Alice a chippy tea each. On me. My treat."

"Oh!" Jenny exclaimed. "A chippy tea? Right. Will you be having some too?"

"No. I've gotta get goin' but, listen, I'll let you get yourself settled in proper like and then I'll see you in a few days. Okay? Busy night tonight. Saturday, and there'll be a lot of 'em out there, especially when all the pubs shut and they'll be feeling randy. That's best time.

105

Anyways, I'll catch early trade first at the bus station, you know, where I first met you? Gosh, it seems bloody ages ago now does that. Anyways, there's always usually somethin' doin' there now at this time."

"Okay, Jimmy, but be careful."

"There you go again, Jen. Telling me to be careful. Told you. I'm Lucky Jim. I can look after myself. Funny, no-one's ever worried about me before 'cept you." He laughed and gave away another one of his cheeky cherub smiles.

"Come on, Jen. Let's go down before your tea gets cold."

Scuttling out of the room and on to the landing he nearly fell over the abandoned bed sheets and curtains that Jenny had forgotten she had left there.

"Bloody hell! Nearly broke my bloody neck!" Jimmy exclaimed, laughing. "What's all this?"

"Oh, sorry, Jimmy. It's to be put outside with the rubbish. Just haven't got round to it yet."

"Oh, I'll do that for you. I'll leave it by the bin when I go out. Okay?"

"Thank you, Jimmy. Are you sure?"

"Yeh, no worries."

Jenny suddenly remembered Alice's old slippers and asked Jimmy if he would not mind taking those too?

Jimmy was quick to respond. He went straight to the bathroom, where Jenny said they had been left. Retrieving the stinky articles and, with arms loaded, he gave Jenny a wink and together they made their way downstairs.

CHAPTER 7

'So many assume, so little know.'

Unknown

'Ruddy Kipper'

Alice was sitting at the dining table. The gas fire had been switched on; its flickering flames actively trying their best to create the warmth that only they could radiate. So far, they were succeeding and Jenny was glad. The standard lamp in the corner was casting a cosy glow around the room. The curtains were still open and the early winter's evening was beginning to draw itself in. A pot of tea and two enamel mugs were sitting on the table along with the 'chippy tea'.

The 'chippy tea', wrapped in newspaper, was going to be a first for Jenny and already the heady, sharp smell, seeping through the printed page, was making her taste buds tingle in anticipation. She had only eaten a bar of chocolate, the one that Jimmy had brought for her earlier that morning, and now her stomach had been stirred into wanting more food. Too many times she had had no option but to ignore what her stomach was telling her and how its sinking emptiness, its gnawing pit would then twist and spread into a cold, ruthless nausea since there was little to satisfy it. Hunger was something she had been used to and had, over the years, learned to cope with its cruel assaults. Yes, a bar of chocolate would have sufficed once. Not any more. There was no need for her ever to be hungry again. No need. No need at all.

Jimmy had already said his goodbyes and Alice had started to pour the tea.

"Come on, lass. Sit down and I'll pour you a cuppa. Help yourself to milk and sugar," she said, pointing to the sugar bowl and a bottle of milk placed unceremoniously next to it. There were no plates or cutlery. Newspaper wrapping and fingers seemed to be the crockery of choice and Jenny eagerly followed Alice's execution of how one proceeded to eat at this meal.

She opened the newspaper wrapping to reveal its contents of battered fish and a portion of chips.

"Tuck in, lass, before it gets cold."

Jenny 'tucked in', savouring every greasy salt and vinegar coated mouthful and thankfully filling the empty space in her stomach.

Alice had soon finished and, after licking her fingers and screwing up the fat soaked newspaper, she sat back on her chair rubbing her stomach. Without any warning she belched out loud. Not once but twice and then heaved a huge sigh of contented relief.

"Oh! Bloody lovely that. Always enjoy a good chippy tea. Can't beat it. Oh heck! Just remembered. Didn't do any bread and butter. How could I forget that? Never mind. Next time."

Despite Jenny's shock at Alice's command of belching in company, and without any embarrassment, or excusing herself, she could not help but smile and nod her head. Alice made her feel settled and unafraid. This was not a place where one stood on ceremony. Far from it and Jenny, not for the first time that day, was glad.

"Well, Jen, think it's been a good day all round. I've had my bath, hair's done, food in our bellies and you've settled yourself in a bit. I'll let my hair dry on its own. It's only fine so won't take long. Nearly dry now. Tomorrow, I might just shove a few rollers in and then a bit of a backcomb and 'Bob's your uncle', as they say. In a bit I'll put some war paint on ready for who might turn up. Shirl should be here around seven and she'll just go straight up to my room. She knows and, like I said, she'll not bother you. Funny bugger. Miserable as sin. Still, she does a good job. Been doin' it for a long time now."

Alice started to pour another cup of tea. Looking at Jenny she held up the teapot, "Want a top up, Jen?"

Jenny nodded.

"You know what they say, Jen? A cup of tea makes everythin' better. So, drink up and enjoy and stop lookin' so bloody worried all the time. You're goin' to be alright here. I'll look after you. I know I came on a bit hard last night but I was just checkin' you out and now I think I've got the measure of you a bit. I have that."

Jenny had not realised that she had come across in this way and felt somewhat embarrassed. She really did not want to look worried or anxious, least of all in front of Alice who had so far been nothing but kind.

"Yeh, Jen," Alice continued. "Yeh. There's somethin' about you, Jen. I can sense somethin' really good and gentle and honest about you. I know you're clever and you're quick. I know you can read. You read the instructions on the box easy enough. I saw that and I definitely know you can clean and make a nice home. Bathroom told me that much. Don't think I didn't notice how tidy and clean it all was because I did.

"Still, I can sense too that you're a private person and a bit of a loner maybe. Am I right?"

Jenny was lost for words and all she could do was acknowledge agreement. Good? Gentle? Honest? How could Alice be so wrong? So very, very wrong. Plaudits far removed from how Jenny saw herself after what she

111

knew she could do. Clever and quick? Commendations her teachers at school would agree with. Yes, she could read and, yes, she could clean. Both of these could be accredited to her without question. Private and a bit of a loner? Well, yes, but then she had had to be.

She looked at Alice and forced a smile as Alice continued to chatter.

"Yeh, Jen. All's good. Do you know? I have all I need and want right here in this house. This place is a bloody palace seein' as where I came from. Meetin' Bert, God love him, and him bringin' me here to look after him, well, I think I've already said about that, but still, him bringin' me here was better than winnin' the pools. Mind you, I wouldn't mind winnin' the pools, that's if I did 'em, and I don't."

Jenny had little notion of what Alice was referring to. The pools? She could only assume it was a raffle of sorts.

With her belly now full, a hot cup of tea in her hands, the warmth of the fire and the peace and quiet held in that time space, she continued listening with interest to Alice's vivid monologue.

"He were a clever man was Bert but, a bit like you, he were a loner. Private man, too. Kept himself to himself. He liked my company, though. Said I were a breath of fresh air and could make him laugh. 'Alice,' he'd say, 'you make me laugh.' Well, he liked nothin' better than sittin' in that there armchair by the fire, smokin' a fag and reading one of his books. Always had his head in a book. Spent hours readin'."

Jenny's interest was caught even more and she knew now for sure that the encyclopedias would have been his.

"Yeh, he liked readin' and he even taught me to read a bit better too. Well, enough to get by as I never had much schoolin'. Anyways, what I'm gettin' at is this. He were tellin' me once about this fella he liked. He liked readin' some of his stuff. He said that this fella reminded him of himself. I could never get my head round this fella's name though. Funny old name. All as I could think of when Bert told me this fella's name was Ruddy Kipper, 'cause it sounded somethin' like that. Yeh, Ruddy Kipper. Bert laughed when I called this fella that. Anyways, Bert said this Ruddy Kipper fella was an in… an in… an in…. Oh, I don't bloody know, the not sleepin' thingy."

"An insomniac?" Jenny asked.

"Yeh, Jen. That's it. An in... thingy. Yeh, that. You're right. Told you, you're bloody clever. Well, Bert said he were one, just like him, and so this fella would go out at night, 'cause he couldn't sleep, and he'd go to these brothels and to places where they'd give you drugs to make 'em all sleepy and make 'em imagine all sorts of things in their heads. From what Bert said it were like a dreamy drug. Bert never did that, though, and he never went to brothels either. He just used to come out to the streets for women and that's how he met me and we got

113

on and, in the end, he brought me here and I've told you the rest. But, what I'm gettin' at is this.

"This Ruddy Kipper fella liked women and girls like us and said we were doin' a job and nothin' else. There's nothin' wrong with it. He lived a lot of his life in India and said that what we do here is just normal there and no-one bats an eyelid. Bert told me that this fella said that our job was, 'the oldest profession in the world'. Yeh, he called it a profession, a proper job, and I liked that.

"Yeh, Jen. It's a bloody job like any other and it's the only one I've ever known. My mum was one and, when I were about nine, she took me with her and that's when it started for me. She were always drunk and so were my dad. He never did a day's work in his bloody life so we had to make money for him. Caught him lookin' at me a few times and once he tried touchin' me so I kicked him right in his bollocks where it bloody hurt. The bastard. Anyways, when I turned sixteen I ran away. Saved some money behind their backs, went into the city, got on a train and it brought me here. As good a place as any and I've done alright. Least, I think so. But listen, Jen. What I want to say is you're not to worry about what goes on here. The ones that come here are regulars mainly and they're easy. They come, they go. They come, they go. Just, 'lie back and think of England', as they say."

Jenny wondered, why England? Still, maybe, she would think of England. England? Another distraction.

Another game to play. She would take each letter in turn and think of a word for each one. E for - empty, and so on. Yes, another mind game. Detachment was key.

"Bloody hell, Jen! Is that the time?"

Jenny looked at the clock on the side cabinet and saw it was nearing six o' clock. They had both been so caught up in Alice telling her story that they had not noticed the time. Jenny had been listening with such intent and was impressed with how far Alice had come and her acceptance of all that had been put in her path. Indeed, Bert had been her godsend and it was clear to Jenny that Alice had loved him in her own way.

"Come on, Jen. Let's straighten up and then you can go and do what you have to do. Now, have you got all you might be needin'?"

Jenny was just about to say she had but then remembered the encyclopedias and hammer and nails. Just as she expected, Alice directed her to 'the cupboard under the stairs' and told her she could take the encyclopedias, with pleasure, and a hammer and nails that she'd probably find in a box on one of the shelves.

CHAPTER 8

'Lalun is a member of the most ancient profession in
the world. In the West people say rude things about
Lalun's profession. In the East, where the profession is
hereditary, nobody takes any notice…'

'On the City Wall', Rudyard Kipling, 1865 - 1936

Time to Act

It was nearly time. Already, the inevitable was going to
begin and Jenny was waiting…

All of Sunday she had spent in carefree isolation
cleaning and tidying the rest of the house. The kitchen's
surfaces were sparkling, the cooker was sparkling, the
window - inside and out - was sparkling, the washing up
had been done and everything put away, the floor had
been swept and mopped, the washing machine had been
located and mastered and even the inside of the

cupboards had been put into germ free order. Order and control. Order and control and Jenny felt somewhat easier. She knew that she had only needed to do the bare minimum and even tried leaving a few pots in the sink. However, instead of experiencing a liberation of choice, since there was nobody there to reprimand her for chores undone anymore, it just made her feel anxious and unsettled and so she proceeded to wash the pots and put them away.

The dining room had been straightforward and so too the stairs and landing. The hoover, though clumsy and cumbersome, had been more than serviceable. Standing on a chair, Jenny had even managed to give the dining room window a clean, inside and out, and all surfaces in the room were soon dusted and polished. Order and control. Order and control and Jenny was happy.

Her chores had enveloped her thoughts, had enveloped her whole being and had kept her focused and driven.

The encyclopedias had been retrieved, along with hammer and nails, and already two make-shift bows held back the curtains in her room. Right now, though, as she waited, one side had been let loose to allow a measure of evening light to enter since Jenny did not want to switch on the lamp. Its homely presence softly casting a glimmer was not in keeping at this time. Its homely presence was for her alone and so too were the golden bars of heat radiating from the electric fire. The fire had been unplugged. The room right now was a place of business. Purely functional; even the sheets had been changed to, what Jenny now called them, her 'work sheets'. Her private sheets were, for the present, neatly folded away, in the wardrobe, and to be put back later when Jenny's work that night had come to an end.

The encyclopedias had been placed in correct volume and alphabetical order and were sitting, proudly displaying their spines, on an old wooden box that Jenny had found in the backyard. With leftover material from the curtains, she had managed to cut out a cover for the box to match. Also resting on the box was a catalogue that had been left out with next door's rubbish. Jenny had seen its glossy cover and bold print. 'Empire Stores', it read. She had quickly flicked through its pages. The catalogue had hardly been touched; its fashions, their colours, and all other offerings, Jenny knew would bring her light relief whenever she so wished. She had claimed it and knew next door would not mind.

Monday morning, and Jenny had devoted that to herself. A rose scented bath and she luxuriated in the heat of the cleansing bubbles. Before that she had twisted her long dark locks over one shoulder and chunked her way through with the scissors to just above shoulder length. With a final strimming of loose strands she had more or less got it straight. She had even managed to create a short fringe and no longer had a middle parting. Following the instructions on the 'Born Blonde' box carefully, she reminded herself of what she had to do and was more than pleased with the outcome. A total transformation. The mirror that she had so far avoided looking into, now reflected a girl she did not recognise at all. So, this was Jenny Smith? Yes, Jenny Smith.

She applied the red lipstick carefully. Never really having noticed before just how full her lips were, the lipstick was easy to curve round the outline of a natural cupid's bow and the plushness of the bottom lip. The overall effect was like a rosebud. A red rosebud. Jimmy's frock choice, although pretty, as he described it, was far too big. However, with one of the belts Jenny had found amongst a vast array of dresses in Alice's wardrobe, she had managed to cinch in the waist and was happy with the result. Alice had told her to have a 'good rummage' in the wardrobe and, just like 'the cupboard under the stairs', she could take what she wanted.

Later, when Jenny went to show Alice the result of her transformation, Alice's reaction said it all.

"Well, bloody hell, Jen, lass. Look at you. Pretty as a picture. You are that. Tell you what, though, you look a bit older than you did when you first came. So, what we'll do is this, 'cause I've been thinkin' about it as well. If anyone asks, and they won't, but if you ever need to say who you are, you can say you're my new live-in help and not long left school. I'm giving you board and lodgings and you look after me since I don't find things easy anymore. How's that? Think that's okay. It's as good a story as any and it's what I used to say about the others that's been here. It's just that they looked a lot older than you, that's all. What do you think, Jen?"

Jenny nodded, "Well, Alice," she said, "I think it's okay. Yeh, I do."

Alice laughed out loud at Jenny's attempt at sloppy English.

"Aye, lass. Bloody hell! Carry on like that and you'll fit well in. You will that."

And so, Jenny was all set and ready. Her command of the local dialect would still need to be practised and there was also one last thing she had decided. She had decided not to dress at all for her night's work. Having to meet, greet and undress would just prolong each visit, each episode. Better to lie on the bed, under the sheet and, once the sheet was drawn back, they would be greeted with her nakedness. Fully exposed for what was to take place.

Her naked body under the sheet awaited a physical contact that she loathed. Before long she heard a muffled exchange downstairs and then footsteps hurrying up to her room. A quick knock on the door and he was straight in. No introduction. Nothing at all. In the night light Jenny averted her gaze. She heard his heavy breathing as he undid his trousers. He drew back the sheet and she felt his close presence as he looked down at her on the bed. She could smell stale tobacco mixed with cheap aftershave. Too much aftershave. Unpleasant and strong.

With eyes now shut tight, she knew that she had to act out a part. She knew she had to speak first and then she could become the emotional iceberg she needed to become to see this episode through. Opening her eyes a fraction and her hands clenched tight by subconscious command, she knew that soon he would be on her. She could sense his eyes boring into her, scrutinizing her naked outline in the shadow of the dark. She had to make sure he was wearing the necessary precaution before the performance could begin. Yes, the performance. She reminded herself that she was the principal director and she was the one controlling the scene.

"Hi," she spoke quietly. "You'll find rubbers in the bowl if you haven't got one of your own."

She pointed to a bowl on the dresser at the side of the bed.

"That's alright, love. Always have my own. Here, let's put it on together."

All part of the act, Jenny knew what to do. Whenever the man in Hell bothered to use one he would make her slide it on for him. Yes, she knew what to do and, sitting up, she turned and felt for the erect member. She felt this man's excitement burning as his breathing became heavier and heavier. Once in place he pushed Jenny back onto the bed and began to satisfy his need for release.

As he thrust and thrust and pounded into her, Jenny looked up at the ceiling, her hands once again clenched by subconscious command. There was no pain, no real discomfort. She never felt pain anymore down there since years of violation had seen to that.

She started her alphabet game, the one she had perfected over the years. The 'England' game she would adopt another time when she had practised it and had become used to any rules she needed to apply. For now, she started to go through girl's names, letter by letter. Her aim was to try and think of names that she had never used before. New place. New names. Not altogether easy but a powerful distraction. 'A...A...A... A for Amelia. B...B...B... B for Bridget and so on. She was thankful that her imagination, and her love of reading, gave her proficiency in this game. Thankfully, it was not long before she felt the usual stiffening of a body on top of her and the gasping pants of personal abandonment and the man was spent.

Without ceremony, he got up, gathering together his clothes and shoes, and left the room. She was grateful that she had only reached the letter G.

The flush of the toilet, followed shortly after by footsteps, this time treading somewhat slowly down the stairs, brought Jenny back into the moment.

She lay there for a little while in the quiet of the room and wondering what to do next. She wanted to go to the bathroom, where she had left the flannel and soap and towel ready to wash away the shame of flesh on flesh between her legs. A shame that she knew she would feel after each invasion.

Eventually, wrapping the sheet around her naked frame, she went to the bathroom. She needed to go to the toilet anyway. She could not hear any voices downstairs so knew that she had time to have a pee at least.

The toilet lid and seat had been left open. The man obviously did not hold with common courtesy and Jenny was not in the least bit surprised. What did surprise her, however, was the abandoned rubber floating on the water as she looked down. Was it meant to be flushed? She did not know. The man in Hell would dispose of his own, whenever he chose to wear one, and Jenny never knew how or where. This one had clearly refused to disappear when she had heard the toilet being flushed earlier. She did not like seeing it there. She wanted it to be gone. It probably still had some of the man's filth in it.

Jenny flushed the chain. She watched the rinse and swirl of the water obscuring, just for a second, her view of the bowl's unwanted content. All to no avail. It was still there! Tearing off a substantial amount of toilet paper, Jenny covered over the item and scooped it up quickly. She put it in the wastebasket telling herself that this would be an issue she would need to address. She washed her hands and then wiped round the toilet seat after putting it back in place before she sat down to pee. As she sat there her mind was thinking of how the used rubbers could be disposed of and wondered what others had done before her. Jenny needed to sort this. She needed order. She needed control. Think. Think

In the end, and it did not take long, she had decided that she would make sure the wastebasket, in her own room, would be in a prominent position, next to the dresser by the bed, with a plastic bag, or paper bag, open and ready, sitting inside to receive the used rubbers and their slime. At the end of the night she would lift out the bag, tie it up and deposit it in the bin outside. Each night's bag would be thrown away and forgotten. Yes, Jenny had found an answer; a solution. Order and control. Order and control. Panic over and Jenny felt better.

 For now, though, she would turn on the charm and, affecting the local dialect as best she could, she would point out the wastebasket in her room and that they could dispose of the used rubber in there. In the meantime she would take even more toilet paper and, just tonight, make a lining for the basket base and so scoop up the unwanted articles at the end. She would then go outside and somehow leave them in the already overflowing bin. Tomorrow she would make sure to establish some order with the bin's contents since it was still days before the bin men came. Maybe she could ask Jimmy to get her some empty boxes from somewhere. There was no doubting that he could.

With all that established in her head, Jenny washed her hands and returned to her room moving the wastebasket from the corner and putting it next to the dresser at the side of the bed.

Lying down and putting the sheet once more over her naked body, Jenny awaited the arrival of her next customer.

It wasn't long before she heard a slow, heavy tread of steps making their way up the stairs and to her room. Once again Jenny squeezed her eyes tight shut before commencement of the inevitable.

He came straight in and was already quite breathless. He switched on the light. Jenny had not accounted for this and had no choice but to look at the man. She found the whole moment of clear observation so very unsettling but then immediately regained control. Once he started to perform she would be able to close her eyes and detach herself completely and was already thinking of a girl's name beginning with the letter 'A'.

"Well, well, well. What've we got here then?" he uttered breathlessly, already undoing his trousers and abandoning his overcoat on the floor. His shirt buttons barely did their job as they looked ready to pop open at any given moment and reveal the bulging stomach inside. Sitting down on the bed to remove the rest of his clothing, Jenny shut her eyes tight. He was fat. He looked bulky. He looked heavy.

She was letting personal thoughts take over. This was not what she wanted. Regaining control was paramount and so she became the emotional iceberg she knew she could become once more.

She opened her eyes and, averting her gaze, she pointed to the bowl on the dresser and quietly, in her now new way of speaking, said, "Hi. If you haven't got your own rubber, there's some of 'em in there. In that bowl. Okay? Yeh, you'll find 'em there."

"Well, love. Thanks. Just need a bit of action before I put it on proper, like. You look at it nice while I pull."

Jenny did as she was told and, before long, he was ready for the rubber to be applied. He was excited and, with his pudgy fingers, he clumsily slid on the protection himself. Jenny lay back and her alphabet game began.

Despite being so fat, Jenny did not feel the weight on top of her and, much the same as last time, he did not take long. One thing Jenny had been trained to do was to make noises that seemed to enhance the man's progress, making him think he was creating a lot of pleasure and so reaching his final stiffening quickly. Yes, in Hell she had been made to perfect noises and had never dared to refuse. At least these noises made the nightmares end more quickly. So, she made them and had learned to separate these fake noises from the games in her head. Multitasking. Yes, multitasking meant control and control was foremost. Control was hers.

As he dismounted, still in performance mode, Jenny uttered, "Okay, then. Hope to see you again sometime soon maybe. There's a bin there for your rubber if you want."

Jenny seemed to have caught the man off guard as he fumbled with his limpness and tried to regain some balance.

"Er, oh, yeh, yeh. Great. Yeh. Bin. Thanks. And, yeh. See you soon. Yeh, I'll see you soon love. I will that."

In the horrible glare of the naked bulb, Jenny affected a smile. She would get a lightshade as soon as she could.

A few moments later the man was dressed and he was gone. Straightaway, Jenny got up and switched off the light and this time, fully exposed, she hurried to the bathroom where the flannel, soap and towel were in attendance

The rest of the night progressed in much the same way and Jenny took a little comfort from the fact that, between each of the visitors, she did have a bit of time to herself and, in a strange sort of way, started to get used to the pattern of events. In fact, none of these men were what she had been used to. They were not brutal or frightening in any way. They did not hurt her or make her feel any pain. One or two, just as Alice had said they might, came only to look and gratify their own needs themselves. As yet she had not been made to put it in her mouth. Something she had always detested. It was too close. It was too near. She would rather endure the pounding and the thrusting. At least it meant she did not have to surrender to the foulness in her mouth. Yes, too close. Still, if she ever had to, she knew she could, as always, programme her thoughts and detach herself. Maybe she would reserve her 'England' letters and words for such times since deep concentration would be needed for 'e' words then 'n' words etc. Maybe she could think of three words for each letter at a time. Triples. Triples for added effect. Yes, a solution and she would be ready.

Ten past midnight and Jenny's work was done. Strangely enough, she had no feelings at all about what she had been doing. It was a 'profession', as Alice had said, just a job, after all. If anything, Jenny had just found it tedious and monotonous. The emotional iceberg could now thaw. It had done its duty. Jenny felt that if all her nights followed a similar pattern then she would continue to direct and manage and she would cope.

She stripped the bed and folded away her 'work sheets'. Leaving the bed bare, and allowing the mattress to air for a while, Jenny made her last visit of the night to the bathroom.

CHAPTER 9

'Hope is being able to see that there is light despite all
of the darkness.'

Desmond Tutu

August 1969

A new life does not just open like a present, with fancy
paper and ribbons and guarantees of comfort and
happiness, but more as a road, with all its twists and
bends and undulations, until something better is finally
reached.

Like the light that its name implied, Beacon Street stood
out from the rest of the warren as this was now Jenny's
home and one that she was thankful for.

Since first arriving time had moved on and the bleak
cold, wind and rain of winter seemed so long ago. The
heady heat of August now crept across the terraced

landscape, igniting the weeds and grasses that grew in between the cracks in the pavements.

Routine and order had firmly established itself and Jenny's night time work had settled into a pattern of events with her usual visitors, their usual wants, their usual behaviours and needs. A few new visitors, every now and again, but none of them threatening or difficult. Alice would monitor their comings and goings and always made sure Jenny had some time to prepare and compose herself between each visit.

The men generally came in through the back kitchen door and Jenny soon discovered that the packet of cigarettes, she had seen that very first night on the mantle, were not Alice's at all but were there for the visitors. Alice had told her that she used to be a heavy smoker but had not touched one in years. She had done well to abstain for so long and was proud of her achievement. The cigarettes were no longer the temptation they once were. Alice would also offer visitors a 'tipple', as she liked to call it; a whiskey or brandy, although confiding that she would often water down the bottles to make the liquid stretch further.

Wednesdays and Thursdays were Jenny's nights off and Shirl would take over. Alice would make sure to direct visitors to the front bedroom, instead of Jenny's, and Jenny knew then that she could settle down comfortably in her own private space. In all this while she had never seen Shirl nor did she want to. Hidden away, Jenny would spend time furthering her education, painstakingly reading through her much valued encyclopedia collection.

Daytime chores were a welcome distraction from any lingering thoughts that would, although not as frequently now, still present themselves without invite from her mental cupboard. Routine meant that the house was always spic and span with the refreshing scent of Pledge polish a permanent feature.

Alice's bath times were taken every Wednesday and Friday afternoons. Alice was perfectly happy with this arrangement and, anything in between, was what Alice liked to call, a 'cat lick', or a 'top to toe' with soap and water. Jenny, on the other hand, was free to indulge in the rose scented bath bubbles as often and as many times as she wished.

Since first arriving in Beacon Street, Alice, as well as Jimmy, had come to mean so much to Jenny. They were an anchor. An anchor that she had never had in her life till now. In Hell she had been drowning in pain, endlessly swimming but never reaching a harbour, a safe harbour. Life was a torture, a torment. Not anymore. Their smiles provided a warmth that had helped rid her of the masks that she had been wearing her whole life and, apart from her night time work, her smiles were now real and liberating.

Wearing her night time mask, and serving the men as she did, was a means to an end providing hope in her heart; the hope that one day, sometime soon, she would be dressing the windows of her cotton candy cottage with the blue and white gingham curtains that she loved. She had already started saving.

Alice and Jimmy could always visit and they could drink tea and eat cake in the garden. She would want them to. Without them knowing it, they had helped so much to keep the box in her mental cupboard at bay, hidden and closed apart from just a few occasions. One such occasion was when, shortly after arriving in Beacon Street, she had overheard two women in the chippy discussing what they had heard in the news. Jenny had been waiting in the queue, for the now customary Friday chippy tea, when she heard them saying that the police were looking for a young girl that had disappeared and that the girl was not local.

"Bloody awful. Shockin' what they found. Yeh, bloody awful. Young girl's disappeared. She could be anywhere. Only a kid."

"Yeh, Val, I know. Shockin'!"

Jenny listened for a moment and knew that, if she took any further notice, she would risk her mental cupboard opening fully and the box inside spilling and spewing out all its contents. She would not allow it to and focused on the sounds of the sizzling fat spitting and swathing the potato chips in a crispy, golden coating. Val's turn to be served and the conversation ceased. The cupboard door was slammed shut once more.

One of the things Jenny had promised herself, when she had first started earning money of her own, was a new coat and it was not long before she was able to go and buy one. Jimmy, however, still continued his regular shopping sprees and, no matter how many times Jenny tried telling him there was no need for him to keep bringing her things, her words simply fell on deaf ears. His eyes would light up whenever he presented one of his acquisitions, be it red lipstick, or a frock (regardless of size), chocolate, sweets and, even one time, a small transistor radio that he said had, 'fallen off the back of a lorry'. Jenny's heart would melt as he looked at her so longingly for approval that she just could not deflate his delight.

Jenny knew it was wrong for him to steal but Jimmy could never understand what difference it made. Right or wrong meant little in Jimmy's world. She knew that and so, to assuage his sprees, she did what she had vowed to do that very first morning waking up in Beacon Street; she went to Jimmy's usual haunts to buy things herself and spend money.

The market soon became one of Jenny's favourite places. Situated right next to the bus station, where Jenny had first met Jimmy, the market was a dreamland of colour and scents and sounds and items of every possible description. She would weave her way through the dense flow of people, drinking in the atmosphere like an elixir. Sometimes, she felt there were not enough hours in the day for her to fully embrace everything the market had to offer. She felt she could be anyone, or perhaps no-one at all, as she flowed along with the people there, never stopping for obstacles in their way but merely swirling around them. She loved the chatter between sellers and buyers and the caricatures of bubbly friendliness as the sellers plied for trade.

It had not taken Jenny long to buy a coat. She had not been in Beacon Street more than a few weeks when she had enough money to go to the market. She had already seen a coat on one of the stalls that was perfectly serviceable. She had paid the ticket price and hurried back to Beacon Street eager to rid herself, once and for all, from association with the coat she still had to wear.

As soon as she had opened the back door, and found the biggest pair of scissors in the top kitchen drawer that she knew were there, Jenny rushed up to her room to begin her long awaited task.

With each laboured cut of the scissors through the thick, woollen fibre and its lining, Jenny felt a release, a final release from a tie that still held her to Hell. The itchy fur collar she left till last. The sweet, cloying smell still faintly lingered, trapped inside and maintaining its vile presence. Now, as she snipped and clipped and cut and cut Jenny smiled wryly. Her past was going. Her past would be no more and, once all the remnants of the coat were bagged and put in the bin outside, it would be gone forever. Dumped. Dumped with the rest of the rubbish. A heartfelt thought. A heartfelt wish, albeit naïve.

CHAPTER 10

'To acquire the habit of reading is to construct a refuge
from all the miseries of life'

W. Somerset Maughan, 1874-1965

Solace

Another go-to place for Jenny, as well as the market,
was the municipal library situated in the centre of town
on The Crescent. The library, magnificent in its
architectural design and craftsmanship, was quickly
appreciated by Jenny's keen eye for detail. Such a
splendid building, it looked more in keeping with
romantic settings such as Florence or Rome or Paris
and not in the centre of some industrial northern town.
Jenny had seen pictures of these beautiful settings in the
pages of her encyclopedias and now felt that she could
actually be anywhere in the world.

Alice had first told Jenny about the library and thought
that she might like it there. Understatement! Jenny's

love of reading held no bounds and the library very soon became her nirvana; her sanctuary. A very special place.

Jenny recalled the very first time she had looked up at the commanding building with its wide stone steps leading to the front doors. Tingling from top to toe with nervous excitement she ventured inside. A hushed silence greeted her emanating the warmth and calm and peace of this wondrous place.

She stood for a moment in awe. Thousands upon thousands of books waiting to speak their words. Books stacked in neat rows on shelves and arranged in order. Books on shelves all aligned back to back where their contents could not be judged by their covers. Solid, sturdy shelves supporting inky treasures; ink on papery leaves that would always remain even though centuries may pass.

Not wanting to draw attention to herself, Jenny made her way towards one of the rows pretending to know exactly what she was looking for. She need not have concerned herself, however. No-one even looked her way, undisturbed and lost in literature and in books that gave answers to questions about the world, about science, about humanity; the heavy words of philosophers and other mysteries that few knew immediate answers to.

This was her first visit to the library and Jenny knew it would not be her last. Unlike the library at school, where she would spend most of her lunchtimes and where, when she was in the juniors, she was a library monitor, this one served a much wider community and Jenny was overwhelmed by all that it had to offer. She wandered slowly up and down the rows just staring at the shelves. She felt it almost sacrilegious to disturb the books carefully arranged with their spines revealing titles and authors and automatically making you tilt your head in order to read them.

Jenny's love of reading had been encouraged by her very first teacher at school. The teacher wore red lipstick and was beautiful and kind and, as Jenny looked at all the magic on offer, she remembered a story her teacher had read out loud to the whole class on more than one occasion. Each time, she sensed a sadness in the teacher's voice and could not comprehend why. Jenny had never actually read through the book herself and wondered if a copy might be found amongst all this wonder. Jenny now had a clearer focus. She had something to look for and her heart started to beat faster. She had wanted to remain inconspicuous. However, she knew she would need to ask for assistance since she did not know who had actually written the book. All she could recall was its title and that the writer had a funny sounding name.

She approached the lady at the front desk and, any misgivings she may have had about being recognised, were immediately dispelled. Jenny was aware that there had been descriptions in the papers about a missing girl from out of town and kept having to remind herself that she was not that girl at all. Jenny was older and was looking after her landlady, Alice. Jenny had short blonde hair and wore a hint of red lipstick even in the daytime. Alice hardly ever read the paper but once, in passing, told Jenny that she never held much store by what the papers reported and that there was always a good reason why people did what they felt had to be done. With that, Alice had poured them both another cup of tea and the bond between them was felt even deeper.

The lady looked up from what she was doing and smiled. There was a kindness in her smile, a gentleness and Jenny felt herself relaxing.

"Yes, can I help you, young lady?"

Remembering her now new way of speaking, Jenny proceeded in her mission. "Oh, yeh. Thanks. If you don't mind?"

The woman's smile widened.

"Not at all. That's what I'm here for."

Jenny's manners were not always required if she were to be totally convincing; something she kept forgetting. Still, the kind lady appreciated them.

"Well, I wa… I were wonderin' if you had a book called, 'The Giving Tree'? Don't know who wrote it, you see, but I know it's a funny name."

"'The Giving Tree', 'The Giving Tree'," the librarian repeated. It took her just a moment before she could remember the book's creator. "Of course," she announced quietly, "Shel Silverstein. Such a beautiful story. Follow me and I'll show you."

It was not long before Jenny was handed over the book. "Thank you very much," she said.

"You're welcome, my dear. The book is a children's story really but adults still like to read it too. Its message is usually lost on young children and it's only when we get older that it comes to mean something. See what you think. If I can help you with anything else, just let me know."

Jenny listened intently and nodded, eager to absorb the book's message for herself and wondering whether this was why her beautiful teacher's voice would often quiver as she read it out loud; a quiver totally lost on her young audience but not on Jenny. She had noticed and now would be able to find out why. Nine years on and Jenny knew she would understand.

Gently running her fingers down the book's front cover, she took her time looking at the squiggly drawing of a tall tree, its top spilling off the page and a tiny boy looking up at it. The squiggly drawings continued in much the same vein on each of the pages telling the story in themselves without hardly the need for words. Such was the skill and talent of the author; the words an added bonus. Simple words but the lady had been right. There was a message. A universal message of selfless love that, even before she had come to the end, made Jenny feel sad. Very sad.

The tree, like a true mother, like a mother should, loves her boy. She gives and gives him everything and more, all through his life, despite getting little in return. Her love is unconditional. Jenny felt sad since she had never known the love of a mother and had never felt it. Her tree had been bare, rotten and damaged. She felt sad since, had she been in the boy's place, she liked to think that she would have appreciated everything given to her and would never have taken anything for granted.

Putting the book back in its rightful place on the shelf, Jenny made to leave and, trying her best to control a slight quiver in her voice, she thanked the librarian and said goodbye.

'Ruddy Kipper' was Jenny's next mission at the library. She wanted to find out the actual name of the author Alice had once been telling her about. She was interested to learn more about him.

Making her way to the rows of 'K' authors, she followed their alphabetical order. She had automatically assumed the forename would begin with 'Rud' and it wasn't long before she discovered the name: Rudyard Kipling. Jenny stifled a giggle at Alice's interpretation of this somewhat strange sounding name. 'Ruddy Kipper' was quite an accomplished writer, judging by the range of books he had penned; each one almost crying out to be taken off the shelf and its contents revealed.

As she browsed the different titles one, in particular, made Jenny look twice. Wide-eyed, she gingerly liberated the text from the shelf. Tracing her fingers over an illustration of Mowgli and the black panther, Bagheera, Jenny felt that this story must have held a much greater meaning that she had possibly overlooked.

'The Jungle Book' had taken Jenny to another one of her favourite places: the Odeon cinema. She had taken Jimmy to see it and remembered the feel good factor the audience was left with as they made their way home. The film had been a musical adventure that had Jimmy singing all the way back to Beacon Street: 'Now I'm the king of the swingers...Oh,oobee doo…I wanna be like you, oo, oo…'. Jenny stifled her giggles at this happy recollection.

Opening the book, Jenny could not wait to start reading and discovering what Rudyard Kipling had really tried to convey on each of its pages.

Whenever, and as often as she could, Jenny's afternoons would be spent in the library where she soon blended into the background. She had her own space, where she liked to sit, and noticed that other frequent visitors had their favoured spaces too. Territorial spaces where, the people that knew about them, would never dare to occupy.

One such space was a table, in the upstairs gallery, where three of the local grammar school girls would like to sit and study once or twice a week after school. From her own vantage point down below, Jenny could just about see them trying to study but oftentimes smothering giggles.

In their brown and yellow uniforms, Jenny was drawn to one of the girls in particular. Leaving the library early one day, she had walked past the girls, with their bulging leather satchels weighing down shoulders, and their happy, carefree camaraderie so clearly obvious. One of the girls saw Jenny and smiled. Jenny noticed, straight away, a genuine warmth about her and, whenever she happened to see the girl again, or catch her eye, the girl would always smile and even sometimes wave. Jenny envied the girl's freedom to learn and her sunny charm and vivacity.

Another time the girl had been leaving early and had not seen Jenny following closely behind. The girl was greeted outside by a woman; an image of the young girl in years to come. The woman beamed when she saw her. This must have been her mother, her 'tree', who flicked a loose strand of the girl's hair behind her ear, exchanged a few words and then, arm in arm, they walked away.

As Jenny watched them disappearing out of view, a wave of sadness washed over her but also comfort in the knowledge that this girl was clearly loved.

On her way back to Beacon Street Jenny decided, right then, to stop off at the market and buy a couple of custard tarts, Alice's favourite, to enjoy together with a cup of tea, before getting ready for their night's work.

CHAPTER 11

"'Now mind yourself,'" he said with a stamp and a fierce glance of his gray eye… "'I'm your Church now! You understand - you've got to be as I say.'"

'Uncle Tom's Cabin' by Harriet Beecher Stowe

Foe

It has been said that time is a thief stealing days away all too soon but Jenny saw it more as a friend guiding her to her final destination, preparing her for her final purpose. Having settled into her new way of life she no longer felt afraid and saw what she did as a stepping stone to her cotton candy life. Her final purpose, her final goal was to live a life of seclusion in a small countryside village away from the hustle and bustle of towns and people, too many people. She would still need a job, however, and dreamed about serving customers in a small village shop surrounded by character and charm.

Jenny had been living in a bubble this past year and she felt hopeful and acknowledged all that she had.

Her night time work was such that she was able to identify certain visitors not just by their voice or their smell, be it aftershave, tobacco, alcohol or sweat, but more by letters of the alphabet. Thankfully, many of them never really got beyond M or N and, only on occasion, someone, other than a regular, might come along and manage a few letters more.

Still, the ability to detach her thoughts in this way had proved invaluable. A coping mechanism that was hers to rule and change as she wished. She had, by now, mastered the 'England' distraction to the point where new words to work with were chosen. At present her word of detachment was 'money', and not because she valued money but that she knew it would one day help to realise her cotton candy dream.

Jenny had been frugal with her earnings. She had already saved quite a significant amount which she kept carefully hidden in a box stored at the back of her wardrobe. She had seen the box one day on the bric-a-brac stall at the market and was immediately attracted to the deep, hand-carved floral and leaf design in the dark wood. It even had a key which Jenny kept in a secret place in her room. It was her treasure box and it was special to her.

Jenny knew she would need to remain in Beacon Street for quite some time yet. Her dream was like being stuck between two realities. One was imperfect but doable;

the other was one she longed for herself but knew its realisation would need very careful planning and order. Order, like everything else, was pivotal. The only thing that would separate Jenny from achieving her dream would be herself. Her mental strength would not allow this to happen. She had come this far and hope kept her driven.

Her birthday had been and gone and, apart from one time, when Alice just happened to mention that Jenny had been there over a year now and must have had a birthday at some point, no more was said. However, Alice was disappointed that she had not been able to celebrate the occasion or make a fuss but Jenny insisted that was how she liked it and that Alice had given her so much already. Still, after one of her weekly shopping trips to the market and local Co-op, Alice had brought back a cake and a huge bar of Cadbury's Dairy Milk - Jenny's favourite.

Jenny was moved and, for the very first time in her life, she felt an overwhelming need to hug another human being. She let her body press in to Alice's warmth. A simple enough gesture, but somehow fragile, and then the feel of Alice's soft, yet strong arms that held her, made Jenny's deep-rooted scars disappear like rain on parched summer earth. A tender yet awkward moment and, at first, Alice was overcome since, despite all the human contact they shared together in private moments, like bath times and washes, there had never been any emotional contact in this way.

147

Disengaging her hold, and coughing once or twice, Alice asked, "Well, Jen, and have you started your monthlies yet?"

Jenny shook her head. She had started to wonder whether there was anything wrong with her and, considering all that her body had gone through from such an early age, she would not have been at all surprised if there was.

And so, Jenny's bubble remained. But, as with every bubble, it had to burst at some point and, without warning, one day it did...

The weather had been miserable and now, as Jenny made her way back to Beacon Street from town, storm clouds threatened to burst from the charcoal grey sky.

She hurried along, not wanting to get caught in the deluge of rain that was imminent. Once the clouds burst Jenny knew that the wind would soon whip the frigid drops of this late February sky and send them hurtling in every direction and then straight down.

An afternoon pot of tea and biscuits with Alice beckoned and Jenny started to run to reach the shelter of Beacon Street before the rain began its onslaught.

She was just in time. As she opened the back kitchen door, the rain poured down bouncing off the flagstones in the backyard and the pavements of surrounding streets.

Fully expecting to be greeted by the usual warmth of the gas fire's flickering flames and Alice already sitting at the table waiting to pour a cup of tea and share biscuits, Jenny was met with nothing. The fire had not yet been switched on, the pot of tea had not been prepared and the biscuits were still in the cupboard.

Cheerless and cold and sombre this was not what Jenny was used to since coming to live here with Alice. Something was wrong; something was not right. Raised voices coming from the front room proved as much.

The chaos and cold of the rain outside now echoed her mind and soul and Jenny did not like it. Disquiet seemed to root her to the spot. She needed to restore the equilibrium that had always made her feel safe in this house.

Looking at the gas fire she moved to ignite its flames. She would set the table and switch the kettle on ready for a pot of tea. All this, however, did not lessen the hostility that was coming from the front room; a room she normally associated with the calming, classical strains of Radio 3.

Making her way to the kitchen she was stopped in her tracks. Hearing a heavy thud and a whimpering cry, Jenny knew Alice was in trouble and she rushed to the front room. Before she could open the door it was opened for her and she was confronted by a huge, menacing figure standing tall and blocking her way. He was laughing.

Jenny looked up. He was big. His skin was the darkest colour of ebony. He glared down at her. His glare was calculating. It unnerved her but she tried her best not to invite this threatening presence into her head. The weight of his piercing, dark eyes, and the smile now beginning to spread further across his chiselled face, he looked at her like a wolf might observe its prey. An air of power, of total confidence that would make one want to back away, but not Jenny. She pushed hard against the man and forced her way into the room. Alice was trying to lift herself up off the floor. Jenny rushed to help.

Alice looked at her trying hard not to appear anguished or upset but nothing could disguise the look of sheer terror in her eyes.

Laughing out loud, the man left the house slamming the front door shut behind him.

Some time later, in the sanctuary of her own room, Jenny was thankful that it was her night off and Shirl had already arrived to begin work. Normally, at such times, Jenny would escape into one of the books she had now managed to acquire. She would buy books from a second hand book store in town where she had her pick of people's unwanted literary texts. Along with the encyclopedias, these books had now found their place on the makeshift table in the corner of Jenny's room. She was currently following the exploits of 'Anne of Green Gables' and living each moment with the plucky, red-headed orphan as she started out, waiting at the train station, for her new life to begin.

One of the things that the book had started to make Jenny understand was that the unlikeliest of people can often turn out to be the finest of friends. Now, sitting alone in the quiet of her room, Jenny thought about her finest of friends, her only ever friends. One, a young boy who sold himself for sex and, the other, a middle-aged woman who earned money from the favours that Jenny sold. Alice and Jimmy meant so much to Jenny. She did not quite realise how much until today and what had happened just hours before.

Jenny had got Alice settled at the dining room table whilst she prepared a pot of tea and the usual offering of biscuits on a plate. Today, custard creams. A choice favourite. With a gentle bite of her lower lip, Jenny would always enjoy splitting her custard cream in half, eating the dry side first and then savouring the half with the cream filling. Not today, though. All she could do was look at them.

As Jenny poured the tea, dread, like some sort of invisible demon, sat heavily on her shoulders and, when Alice declined a custard cream too, the weight intensified until all was revealed.

Alice started to explain who the man was and what he was doing there. The man's name was familiar and Jenny recalled Jimmy once mentioning who he was. The man was Troy. He ran a card school and drinking establishment exclusively for the Afro-Caribbean community although white men, that could afford it, were often allowed in. The police would turn a blind eye to the illegal goings on since Troy had a few of them in his back pocket and they would ignore his activities and get paid for the privilege. This suited Troy who now also owned a number of girls working the streets. They would work from his club when he wanted them to. His business and influence was growing by the minute.

The landlord, that Alice always referred to as the 'greedy bastard' and a 'bloody crook', had now gambled away practically all he owned, including some of the houses on Beacon Street. He had informed Troy that a lot could be made from Alice, and what went on in the house, and now Troy had come to tell her the house was his. He was increasing the rent and, whenever he wanted, he would come and take what was on offer for free. Alice had tried to argue with him since the increase was quite a sum. It would mean maybe having to work two girls at once. She did not want to do this since the relatively low profile they had, and that had been established over the years, could be at risk. Troy had also said that what went on should be all day, everyday. He was heartless and cruel and did not care how Alice was going to get round this. If she could not then he would throw her out and, anything worth taking, would be his. Jenny included.

Alice had tried to argue and come to some alternative arrangement but was met with a slap and a firm instruction of never to answer back to him again.

Alice had told Jenny not to worry and that she was already forming a plan. However, from the look on her face and the sadness in her eyes, Jenny thought that Alice was not altogether convinced of any resolve she was trying to form in her mind.

Lost in their thoughts, biscuits still untouched, Jimmy had come bursting through the back door, soaking wet. So much had happened since Jenny's earlier escape from the deluge, still crying down outside, only to find a flood of fear and destruction now threatening to drown and destroy her safe haven. They were not drowning yet, though. Together they would weather this storm even if it meant moving to somewhere else.

In all the while Alice had been explaining things to Jenny, she told her that, even though Beacon Street had been her home, her refuge, her domain for so long, she was thinking that moving might have to be an option. They could set up somewhere else. Another side of town, away from this end, where Troy and his cronies were fast becoming key figures.

Jenny held onto the idea of moving and Alice told her she would go and make some enquiries at shops out of the area to see if anything was being advertised in their windows. She would get a bus tomorrow over towards Varley Street and thereabouts. Cheaper accommodation may not have the 'luxuries' of Beacon Street but they would cope and, with Jenny's flair and imagination, they would make it work. They would make it comfortable. They would make it theirs and all would be right once again.

The road to one's dream is never easy and oftentimes laden with unforeseen obstacles. Jenny saw this as just an obstacle, an obstacle that, together, they could overcome. With this in mind, Jenny felt better and in control. There was hope.

All the while Jimmy had been listening intently and later, when he made to leave, his parting words were, "Don't worry, Jen. I won't let that fuckin' crazy bastard hurt you or Alice. I promise."

As he spoke, crumbs were spitting forth from his mouth and, when Jenny looked down at the plate on the table, the custard creams were all gone.

CHAPTER 12

'Pain can be controlled; you just have to disconnect it.'

James Cameron - Filmmaker and Environmentalist

But What Happens When You Can't?

After the unforgiving clouds that had covered the sky for days, the sun had, at last, decided to shine down on this northern town and give it a much needed break. Since Troy's unwelcome intrusion a few days before, Jenny had decided not to go out, preferring to remain in Beacon Street with Alice should she need her. Jenny felt more than ever that Alice would be safer with her being there. Troy was a bully and together they would stand up to him. Jimmy, too, had been round every day to make sure they were fine, each time bringing ample reserves of sweets and chocolates. Jenny had long since given up trying to tell him there was no need for his sugary supplies, albeit Jenny's favourites.

All three of them knew it was only a matter of time before Troy resurfaced and Alice had acted quickly. She had already been to Varley Street and its surrounding area - a not altogether favourable one but still far enough away from Troy's domain. There had been a few properties advertised in a couple of the local shop windows and Alice had arranged a viewing of two of them with Jenny. The rent was affordable and they needed to get away as soon as possible. They had another three weeks before Troy's rent was due. Alice would make sure to leave what was owed so that he had no call to come looking for them. Should he return, as he said he would, for time with Jenny, then Jenny had resolved to play her part, detach herself, disconnect herself from an act her body had now been programmed for and prayed he would satisfy himself quickly and he would not hurt her. She was prepared. Fully expecting him to come in the evening for sex, as was the usual, Jenny had not envisaged or considered any different. Mistake. A big mistake…

Alice had gone to visit her friend, Aggie, next door but one, for a chat and tea and biscuits and no doubt telling her confidante all about the imminent move. Fortunately, for Aggie, hers was not one of the houses that Troy had acquired. Jenny liked Aggie. Widowed now for quite some time, she was a true friend to Alice;

a generous, kind lady, meek and shy who kept herself to herself.

Sitting comfortably on her bed, and with pillows propped, Jenny started to turn the pages of 'Anne of Green Gables', to where she had last read, and to continue Anne's life journey, when she suddenly heard a key turning in the front door lock. Jenny thought Alice must have forgotten something, since she had not been gone long, but then wondered why she had not come in through the back kitchen door which was never locked? Footsteps were hurrying up the stairs and, from the sound, she guessed two steps at a time. Long legs. Not Jimmy's.

It was still early afternoon and, other than Jimmy, no-one ever came up the stairs at that time of day to see her. She felt her skin prickle and knew, from her previous life, the one in the box way back in the deepest recesses of her mental cupboard, that this presaged something terrible. She was not ready. She was not prepared. Wrong time of day. Wrong sheets on the bed. No rubbers to hand. Everything was put away. She was clothed. This was not the time. Fear, panic and dread, all visceral, trickled down her spine as she knew exactly who this must be. Clinging on to 'Anne of Green Gables', Jenny looked at the door. Motionless, rigid, her gaze now fixed, she waited for it to open.

A bold, deliberate, provocative entrance. No knock; his towering presence loomed as he had already started to unzip and remove his trousers.

She had to compose herself but, before she could even try, she knew she was back in Hell when he demanded that she turn over. Like the little frightened girl she used to be, Jenny did as she was told. Alphabet game? Alphabet game? Control. Control. All to no avail as his coarse, whiskey tongue was, before she knew it, licking at the skin on her neck and his strong hands pushing and crushing her face into the pillow. Suffocation. A godsend but God had never sent his help when she had been in Hell so why would he now? She knew she would have to tolerate the forced torture she thought she had long since escaped.

His chin rested on her shoulder then his lips clamped down on her ears, one at a time. They were light at first and then he started to bite. Jenny squirmed, eyes clamped shut. The teeth turned to his tongue sliding down the rim of each ear. Sitting astride her, his bulk held her, fixed, as he slid his hands down her sides stopping at her waist. He lifted up her dress and felt the inside of the elastic waist of her knickers before yanking them down. One hand on her neck again she felt his breath as his mouth nipped at the tender skin. Her skin bruised so easily she knew it would make a mark. His lips began to suck at the skin furiously now, until Jenny managed to move her face and breathe out a noise; a scream of panic and hurt she did not register as coming from her. It seemed removed. Distant.

"Hush now you little bitch. You hush now, hush now," he panted, as he held her neck down.

She tried to fight the panic that was pushing up from her chest like a choking tide. The panic rising, her breath bunched and gathered and Jenny wanted to drown. She wanted to pass out. It would at least save her from what she knew this beast was going to do. She choked down the rising bile, consciously flexing her hands and feeling the pain of her nails digging into her palms. Then, an intimacy that was disturbing and discomfiting and one she thought she had left in Hell paralyzed her. It was just as Jenny remembered. The waves of pain, acute pain, stinging pain, started their crashing momentum as he brutally penetrated a private part of hers that had already been sodomised in Hell; a part she had vowed would never be touched again.

Caught up in his lustful attack, he released his hold on Jenny's neck and she released another scream; a rageful, frightening scream and all she wanted to do was shut herself down in a foetal position to protect herself.

She heard the scream again. Her scream. Her scream of unrelenting pain as he drove in hard to satisfy himself. He pounded into her, over and over, faster and faster and then a voice, a familiar voice, shouting, interrupted the pounding.

"Leave her alone! Get off her, you fuckin', crazy bastard! You fuckin', dirty bastard! Get off her! Leave her alone!"

Jimmy had heard Jenny's screams from outside in the backyard and had burst onto the scene, punching his little fists into the beast's back to stop his attack on Jenny.

Half naked, Troy's penis, no longer the erect vile member of so much hurt, was now fully exposed as he tried to fight off Jimmy. Like a rag doll, Jimmy was flung across the room. Trance-like, Jenny watched as Troy reined in blow after blow, punch after punch, kick after kick while Jimmy cowered trying to protect himself. Kick after kick, punch after punch, blow after blow. He did not stop.

Abject fear and shock generated anger, a blind, uncontrollable fury and violence that Jenny had felt and experienced just once before. As if lost in a horrific nightmare, Jenny scrambled to open the dresser drawer, retrieving the scissors that had last been used to cut the pretty material Jimmy had once got for her, and she launched her attack on this foul man.

The first stab into the smooth, glistening, ebony skin of his back caught him off guard and then she stabbed again. She stabbed and stabbed and stabbed away at the hurt he had inflicted on Jimmy. She stabbed and stabbed and stabbed away at the hurt and the worry he had inflicted on Alice. She stabbed and stabbed and stabbed away at the hurt he had inflicted on her. She stabbed and stabbed and stabbed away at the mess he had brought into their lives. She stabbed and stabbed until there was no more left to stab. Done. A bloody heap.

She let the scissors fall and kicked the bloody mess out of her way as she went to wake up Jimmy. He was sleeping. Yes, he was just sleeping. Just as well, Jenny thought, as it meant he would not have felt Troy's kicks and blows and punches. Yes, just as well.

Jenny tried to lift him up off the floor but instead carefully dragged his little, broken body over to the bed. She managed to lift him onto the bed where she settled and cradled her sleeping friend, her angel, her saviour. Like a babe in arms, Jenny held him gently, cradling him backwards and forwards, backwards and forwards, backwards and forwards. He would wake up soon. He would wake up soon. Yes, he would wake up soon.

Backwards and forwards, backwards and forwards she started humming in a quiet, lullaby fashion; the same tune slowly, slowly, over and over, cradling and rocking backwards and forwards, backwards and forwards. Jimmy's favourite song; a happy, lively, carefree 'Jungle Book' moment. Happy, lively, carefree just like Jimmy. Yes, just like Jimmy.

"Oh, oobee, doo... Oh, oobee, doo... Oh, oobee doo…I wanna be like you oo oo..." The same few words, like a broken record, "Oh, oo bee doo…" very, very, slowly, very, very slowly, over and over, cradling and rocking backwards and forwards, backwards and forwards...

WEDNESDAY, FEBRUARY 8th, Angie Ross, missing for over a year, and wanted in connection with the deaths of Dr. John Arthur Ross and Mrs Lucinda Ross, was found in a back bedroom on Beacon Street along with the bodies of 12-year-old James Lomas and 39-year-old Troy, Vincent Emanuel. Angie Ross is currently being held in a secure unit undergoing further investigation pending trial...

PART TWO
CHAPTER 13

'Darkness cannot drive out darkness; only light can do that. Hate cannot drive out hate; only love can do that.'

Martin Luther King Jnr.

May 1970

Having been appointed by the court to determine the psychological functioning of Angie Ross and the circumstances leading up to her offences, I had come this far. Circumstances leading to the death of Troy Vincent Emanuel I now had a clearer understanding of. However, circumstances leading to the deaths of Dr. John Arthur Ross and Mrs. Lucinda Ross had yet to be addressed. There was still some way to go and the case against Angie Ross was ongoing.

The eventual epiphany, the revelation of what she was driven to do that afternoon in Beacon Street was difficult to hear. Since our very first meeting together and, up until this point, I had gained her trust and, as this stage of her story continued to unfold, she constantly reminded me to write it down like a piece of literature, as if this somehow made her separate from its reality. All the way through my drafting of her story, and its process, she would stop, now and again, and ask which word or words did I think best suited what she was telling or trying to say. Together we would discuss words and their alternatives and she would nod approvingly or shake her head in deep thought. All part of the therapy, all part of the whys and wherefores, albeit unusual, I indulged her in the writing of the story and would continue with the process when and if she wanted me to.

In all our sessions together she had often referred to Hell, a place she had once known and had escaped from. Such a fierce word often used to threaten children if they were naughty and one to send shivers down a young child's spine so that they were never naughty again. All make-believe but, for someone little, the threat of a fiery demon, with wings reaching far and wide to swallow them whole, usually had the desired effect. Well, at least until the next misdemeanour. All part of growing up. Not for her. Angie's Hell had been real but, as yet, she had only offered glimpses of it since her mental cupboard, and the box hidden far back in its deepest, darkest recesses, was still closed.

Listening to her account of that fateful, February afternoon in Beacon Street had not been easy since I had felt each moment of her personal pain but had to remain empathetic and remember my professional role.

I knew then, however, as she spoke, she was already starting to withdraw into herself and it would not have mattered how I reacted. She would not have been aware and, as such, had not offered any more of herself for the rest of the session. She had shut down, trapped in her own thoughts.

I knew that this part of her story had come to an end, her life as Jenny Smith, the alias she had given herself as she escaped who she really was and what she had done to make her run away in the first place. Angie Ross needed to emerge now and face her demons in order to heal.

People tended to just see the result of trauma rather than its origins. Angie had yet to reveal its origins and continue her trust in me once more to listen and not to judge.

In our next session together, as expected, I was met with silence. I sensed the loss she felt of a young friend that she was so fond of. The enormity of what she had done to Troy Vincent Emanuel I knew did not resonate fully and was something she did not feel guilty about.

With my 'toolbox' of techniques to hand, I endeavoured to get her to open up once more and speak to me.

I had acquired a copy of 'The Giving Tree', not long after she had very first mentioned it to me, and thought that now it might prove a useful aid. I was right.

As I started to read it out loud to her, a raised eyebrow told me that she was listening. She could hear me.

Just as she had once told me about the beautiful lady, her teacher wearing the red lipstick, I too, when I first read the story for myself, was moved by its poignancy. The poignancy and intrinsic meaning of the story was felt all the more when the simple yet effective words were read aloud. A repressed quiver in my voice, as I reached the story's conclusion, had an effect and, at last, she moved her head and looked directly at me. Breakthrough.

"You can cry, you know. I won't mind. I told you it was sad. Do you see what I mean? He isn't grateful is he? He isn't grateful but the tree never stops loving him and giving him everything. Do you think he knew how lucky he was to have had his own giving tree? Do you? Do you?"

She had caught me off guard and I took a second or two to reply.

"Well, do you?"

"Yes, Jenny, I do. I think that, in the end, he knew."

"Jenny? Jenny? I'm not Jenny. My name is Angie. Yes, my name is Angie, Angie Ross."

She looked at me intently, nodding and nodding her head as if awaiting my acknowledgement and acceptance of who she really was. It mattered.

Smiles have power. They often reach places that the sun cannot, to ease the soul and pierce through the darkness within and so, smiling gently, I looked at her, trying to lighten the burden that I knew she carried and, at last, was hopefully ready to offload. Still nodding, she tried to smile back; a little smile with a slight twist like the smile of a small child determined not to cry. A final, purposeful nod and I knew that Angie, Angie Ross was ready to open the door of her mental cupboard and, from its deepest, darkest recesses, bring out the box that she had kept hidden. It did not take her long.

"Rosie? I can still call you Rosie can't I or would you prefer Susan?"

"Which do you prefer?" I asked.

"I still like Rosie."

"Okay then, Angie, Rosie it is. I like Rosie, too."

"Okay, okay," she nodded and our firm strand of connection was once more established.

"Okay then, Rosie. How would you describe the smell of poo?"

"Sorry?" I asked, nonplussed. "The smell of poo?"

"Yes. The smell of poo. You know? The smell of shit? I need you to get it right for the story. My story."

"Oh, okay. So, you want me to carry on writing a story?"

"Yes, like you were doing before. Like something you'd read in a book with all the proper words and descriptions."

"That's fine. I will do," I assured her. "So, then, why the smell of poo?"

"The smell of poo. Yes, I was about five years old when she took me to school for the first time. Yes, the very first time."

And so, Angie's story, her wanting to share in the creation of words that would help to navigate her tragic world and her memories, began.

I had already caught moments of Angie's Hell when she had momentarily allowed their escape from her hidden box; a glimmer of the life she had been born into. A life behind the closed doors of a grand house in an affluent area some twenty or so miles away from Beacon Street. A road of beautiful houses with manicured lawns and flowerbeds filled with flowers that bloomed in their rainbow of colours according to the seasons. Houses with their sweeping drives and expensive cars parked outside. A road so very far removed from the warren of terraces in Beacon Street. Who knew, however, what went on, what lurked behind these seemingly perfect facades?

A door was now about to open allowing me to step inside one of these houses: the home of Dr. John Arthur Ross, Mrs. Lucinda Ross and their daughter, Angie Ross.

Prior to my very first meeting with Angie, I had already received background information on Dr. and Mrs. Ross and what had been generally known about them. In their investigations the police had not managed to find out a great deal since the Ross' had generally kept to themselves and had few, if any, close friends. The house had been the former home of the late Mr. and Mrs. Albert Henry Parkes who had died tragically in a car accident, driving home one night from an annual gala dinner, leaving their only child, Lucinda, aged just eighteen at the time, sole heir to the Parkes' fortune. Parkes Enterprise, having dealt with the manufacture of steel components for generations, was then left in the hands of partners, Messrs. Flynn and Sons, to run. From police interviews with people that had known the late Mr. and Mrs. Parkes, it would seem that Lucinda was happy to benefit from the spoils of her parents' untimely demise, never having been really close to them in the first place. Aged eighteen, she had chosen to remain living in the family home and, not long after, had met and married Dr. John Arthur Ross, seventeen years her senior. A year later Angie was born.

Like Lucinda, Dr. John Arthur Ross was also an only child who had lost both parents. He was a very young boy at the time and was left in the care of an ageing aunt who, it was believed, doted on him.

Serving in the Royal Army Medical Corps meant that, for much of the time, it was just Lucinda and Angie on their own until 1965 when Dr. John Arthur Ross left the army and took up a position as GP in a practice near home.

A family unit at last. Angie Ross was 10 years old.

CHAPTER 14

'Loneliness and the feeling of being unwanted is the
most terrible poverty.'

Mother Teresa, 1910-1997

Angie 1960 - Age 5

Back then, at five years old, Angie remembered her life
as being a horrible time but just how horrible, how
abnormal, was never realised until she went to school.
Her five-year-old self simultaneously feared and craved
her mother's attention and her recollections, as she
shared them with me to pen like a piece of literature,
were very telling.

Angie's dreams allowed her to put her small hands on
the bars of her cell and push. With a prayer, she would
push and push with all her might to open its door. In

her dreams she would grow stronger and stronger and would find that, from the outside, her cell, her prison, was tiny and pathetic. After so long crouched and cowering in the gloom, she could stand up. She could run and run and let the light warm her skin and her hair flow freely in a heavenly wind. Like a Walter Mitty character she could be whoever she wanted to be and do whatever she wanted to do. She could stand tall and strong and conquer the world. She could sing and dance and play. She could be a pretty little girl, full of sunshine and glow and not ugly, hideous and vile. She could be loved and cherished. Her little body, cradled and nurtured in the arms of a mother that could make this little girl's fears, trapped inside like crystals in a stone, lose their keen sting.

All dreams. Just dreams. At five years old, Angie was happy never to have to wake up again and be forever able to live in her dreams. Reality was a nightmare and it frightened her. Dreams and reality, she was still too young to make real her dreams and escape the dread each new day brought with it. This morning was no exception.

"Get up! Come on! Get up! Get washed and then put these on!"

 Her mother threw a heap of clothes onto the bed. Angie had never seen them before. Like an icy chill numbing her brain, panic, confusion and dread crept over her and, for a moment, she could not move. Cold, glaring eyes looked down at the little girl who knew not to distress her mother in any way. Angie was not a stranger to the dread she was made to feel on a daily basis wondering how her mother would be with her and what she would make her do. Generally, she was left alone in the bubble of her bedroom and away from her mother's erratic mood swings; her volatile mood swings.

Her mother now screamed at her startling Angie into action, "I said, out of that bloody bed now and get a move on, or else!"

Knowing best not to antagonise her mother further, Angie did as she was told. Her mother's frosty stare watching her every move, Angie went to get clean knickers and a vest from one of the dresser drawers.

"Stop!" her mother barked.

Angie froze. She could not have done something wrong already?

"You won't be needing knickers. You've got new ones. Uniform knickers," she said, pointing a perfectly manicured finger towards the bed. "Bloody uniform knickers! Who the fuck cares? Nothing changes. I had the said same uniform knickers too.

"Now, before you put them on go and have your wash. Make sure you wash between your legs and behind your ears and everywhere else. Then, your teeth. Properly, mind. I'll be watching."

Dread and fear locked Angie's stomach tight. She was confused. What exactly was a uniform and why had her mother, so unceremoniously, thrown one on the bed? She knew, however, not to ask questions.

Having very little command of language and vocabulary, Angie was more familiar with just making sounds and signs. She had never had the company of little friends to play with and learn from. Angie had a mother who just barked instructions, shouted at her and, when she was not doing that, ignoring Angie was the norm. Any attempt at communicating and trying to ask something resulted, more often than not, in a slap, then another and another depending on mood. Acquiescence was best and so Angie made her way to the bathroom.

She brought out the little stool at the side of the sink where she had last left it. Angie's stool so that she could reach the sink and not struggle with the taps.

"Tap on the right! I'm watching. Cold water, remember. Cold water always. No point wasting hot water on the likes of you! Now, get a move on. All over wash and then brush your teeth."

It was always the same. Angie would wash herself under the careful scrutinization of her mother except on the days her mother never bothered to get out of bed, which was quite often and Angie was left to look after herself. Still, she would always make sure to try and wash herself properly and remember never to shut the bathroom door. The bathroom door was to remain open whenever Angie was using it, or else. She never knew when her mother would be lurking in the shadows ready to pounce and, too many times, she had been on the receiving end of cruel slaps and kicks. At five years old, Angie was always on her guard. Today, though, just like Tuesdays and Fridays when Judita, the housekeeper, came, her mother was up and ready and, apart from the new clothes called a uniform, with matching knickers, that Angie was going to be wearing, her mother had not revealed any more.

Trepidation swelled within her tiny frame as she was stirred from her thoughts by her mother's mean tone.

"Now, stop dawdling. You're done. Put the towel in the wash basket and get the cloth for wiping round. You know what to do. Make sure the sink is dry and sparkling, or else! Hurry up! Hurry up!"

Under her mother's watchful eye, Angie knew exactly what to do and, within seconds, the sink was dry. Not a splash. Not a stain. Even the soap had been wiped over and now rested on an equally pristine dish; the cloth added to the contents of the wash basket. Yes, Angie knew exactly what to do. She had been trained well and knew the sharp bite of her mother's slap if she failed to please.

"Right, you need to get yourself dressed now so, come on, hurry up! Look sharp!"

Commands and orders. Commands and orders. This is all her mother ever did. She never spoke to Angie other than to issue directives and commands and orders like some military general instilling strict discipline and authority. Angie had never known the tender, gentle tones of a mother's voice or the warmth and grace of a mother's love. Instead, living in a grand house and surrounded by wealth and luxury, Angie felt very lonely, isolated and always, always nervous and afraid whenever her mother was nearby. Her mother would buy her pretty clothes to wear and expensive toys to play with. Angie coveted the toys hoping that, each time she was given one - a teddy, a dolly, a colouring book, crayons and other pleasures, it meant her mother loved her and cared for her. Her mother's contrary behaviour, however, just left Angie bewildered. All she wanted was for her mother to love her and speak nicely to her but she never did. She never did. From the moment she could walk, Angie was charged with caring for herself. It seemed that Angie was a nuisance, an inconvenience, a responsibility interfering with her mother's time. Unlike the dolls her mother played with when she was a little girl, Angie was not a doll that she could discard, abandon when she grew tired or bored. No, Angie was real. Dolls never had wet beds or wet nappies. Dolls never cried or needed feeding. Dolls never needed looking after.

Tuesdays and Fridays were the only times her mother took any notice of her and only because she had to. It was all part of the sham and show. Tuesdays and Fridays meant Judita's comforting presence within an otherwise hostile place. Tuesdays and Fridays meant there was singing in the house, Judita's singing; it meant her mother did not call her names or slap her, reprimand or spy on her. The cupboards and the fridge would be stocked up with food since one of Judita's housekeeping duties included doing the shopping. She would shop on Tuesday and arrive with all the bags, first thing. Angie would be up and waiting, eager to be in her company as she emptied the bags and put their spill of contents away. Said contents were rarely afforded Angie as her mother never cooked, preferring to give her daughter a bar of chocolate, an easier option. Still, Angie did not mind. Anything to assuage the gnawing pangs of hunger, when they attacked, was welcomed. Her mother's sham was expertly employed to the point where she would always make sure the cupboards were depleted in time for Judita's next visit. She would hide away the contents in the bin and make sure to cover them over with other rubbish. Money was no object. Such waste and Judita never found out.

Judita's presence meant a sandwich and a glass of milk and sometimes, when she had the time, it meant her signature dish, lasagne. Judita would always say, "I make you lasagne. I do proper way. Just like Mama and my Nona used to make. Deliziosa," and she would smack her lips together and blow a kiss with her fingers. Angie's excitement at the mention of Judita's lasagne, 'just like Mama and Nona used to make', knew no bounds. The melted cheese and tangy, peppery tomatoes, with their pasta sheets on a plate, was devoured with relish. There would always be more than enough left over to warm up again for later but, once

Judita had gone home, Angie knew she would never see the lasagne again. Her mother would rather throw it away than go to the bother of warming it up and giving it to her daughter.

All the while Judita was there, Angie would enjoy watching her at her chores in the kitchen and around the house and she had the freedom to do so. In company, Mrs. Lucinda Ross played the part of doting mother, loving and kind, most convincingly. In the kitchen she would sit next to Angie, sidling up to her. Angie did not like it. It unnerved her. It unsettled her but still she knew she had to smile. Prompted by the pinching and digging of her mother's nails into the soft flesh of her leg under the table, Angie had no choice. A powerful prompt that Angie knew better than to ignore. Her mother's affected show of devotion was always enough to satisfy Judita of the 'lovely' family she was employed by but, for Angie, it just made her sad. Sadness was her albatross lying like dirty snow over all her emotions and greying her spirit, tainting all that she could ever wish in her life. A 'lovely' family? If only Judita were there to see the night times, true darkness, when Mrs. Lucinda Ross would sometimes come into her daughter's bedroom intent on her next power fix. A drunken victory was always a foregone conclusion; an ego boost at this little girl's expense. Toxic, venomous, poisonous words would be whispered into Angie's ear and, not just the words, but the sweet, sickly, cloying smell of alcohol would make Angie cower and want to be sick.

"Hello, ugly," she would slur. "Hideous, ugly little girl. What are you? Hideous, ugly, vile little girl. Yes, you are... What are you?... Well, what are you?"

Angie knew what was expected of her and she would try to form the correct pronunciation of each of the words. She had heard them so many times before and always endeavoured to deliver them as best she could. She knew she was ugly, hideous and vile. Yes, she knew. Perhaps if she was not then her mother might, just might, love her. Instead, feeding off her daughter's innocence and fear like a sap sucking insect on new spring growth, she would leave the room laughing and energised and buzzing ready to pour the rest of the vodka bottle's liquid waiting for her in the living room. She was her daughter's bully making her feel like some vapid creature. Insipid, colourless, nothing. Nothing. Unwanted and unloved.

"Right. Your uniform. Put it on."

Angie knew how to dress herself but this outfit was different and she felt anxious. She did not want to get anything wrong. Her mother was watching her very closely.

"Well, what are you waiting for? Vest and then knickers. Remember to tuck the vest into your knickers. Your uniform knickers. I had to buy a few pairs and I shall put them in the knickers' drawer later."

Angie put on her vest first then the uniform knickers. The knickers were not pretty, just functional. A dark green colour to match the dark green cardigan and the dark green that she saw in a long piece of material with yellow stripes, like a snake lying comatose, on her bed. Angie wondered what it was.

"Right, now the shirt. Hurry up!"

Horror of horrors! Buttons! Angie was unaccustomed to fastening buttons and certainly not quickly enough for her mother. She need not have worried, however, since her mother was ready with an instruction.

"Line up the bottom button first to the bottom hole and that way you will get them in the right holes. Fasten from the bottom up. Do you understand? Well?"

Angie nodded slowly and proceeded to put each arm in turn inside the sleeves and, fumbling at first, she soon got the measure of the buttons as they slipped into their holes where they belonged and all, thankfully, in correct alignment. The pleated grey skirt was next and Angie made sure that the shirt was tucked well inside the elasticated waistband. She was about to put on the dark green cardigan but was halted by her mother moving quickly over to the bed. Bracing herself, Angie awaited the smarting sting of her mother's slap but could not think what she had done wrong. It did not matter anyway. Her mother would often slap her whenever it suited leaving Angie bewildered and confused and wanting to cry. The slap, however, never came. Instead, her mother picked up the snake-like piece of material, with its yellow stripes against a dark green skin, and held it up.

"Fucking hell!" her mother moaned. "I hated my fucking tie. Well, I'll tie yours this once in a way where you will never need to tie it yourself if you do as I say. I hate having to tie a tie. So, take heed."

Not a snake but a tie and a tie was tied. Her mother put the slither of material round her own neck and crossed one side over another and, after that, Angie was lost. Her little brain in overdrive, concentration shot and her heart beating faster she dreaded having to perform this action under her mother's watchful glare.

"Right. I have tied it ready for you to put on in the future without having to tie it yourself. Now, watch carefully."

Angie watched carefully as instructed. She watched very carefully as her mother started to loosen the tie but leaving enough of an aperture to be able to remove it, from over her neck, and without having to restore it to its snake-like semblance.

"Right, come here."

Angie did as she was told and, without undoing the tie, her mother proceeded to put it over Angie's head and showed her what to do next with the collar and pulling and positioning the tie neatly in place underneath it.

"Right, quickly now so I'll know you will get it right in the future. Take the tie off like I showed you."

Trying her best not to panic, Angie did as she was told and loosened the tie just enough to allow her to put it over her head.

"Right, now put it back over your head and under your shirt collar and then pull it and tighten it into place like I showed you. Then put your collar over it."

Angie did exactly as she was told.

"Fine. Now put the cardigan on and fasten the buttons. Remember to start bottom up. Look sharp!"

Trying very hard to control her trembling fingers Angie, once again, did as she was told.

"Now the socks. Knee length. One thing I always liked. My knee length socks."

Angie did as she was told. Grey knee length socks with two dark green stripes around the tops and Angie liked them too.

Finally, her mother pointed to the end of the bed. A pair of shiny black leather shoes to complement Angie's smart uniform awaited. Shoes with buckles. Still, Angie knew how to fasten buckles. Her very first pair of Clarks red leather buckle fasten shoes had been eventually mastered under her mother's direction and these high shine beauties would be no problem. Angie loved them and was starting to embrace her new uniform. She hoped, though, that having been shown once how to don her new attire her mother would not have to supervise proceedings again.

Angie was always quick to learn and, even at five years old, she already knew that, whatever mistakes she might make with the uniform in the future, she would do her best to rectify them herself without having to bother her mother. She had been on the receiving end of too many reprimands before and usually for nothing at all. Mistakes with the uniform would just be an open invitation for her mother's onslaughts; nasty, vicious jibes leaving a very young girl puzzled and afraid and unhappy. Always the same scenario - 'You silly girl. Stupid, silly girl. Hopeless. Hopeless. What are you? Yes, what are you?'

Too young yet to understand the notion of a rhetorical question, Angie would always try to answer and agree that yes, she was, a stupid, stupid, silly, hopeless girl. Her attempt at speech and her poor enunciation would often result in her mother's cruel laughter and nasty retort, 'See, what did I tell you? Stupid, silly, hopeless. Hopeless!'...

Of course there were things a five year old could not really do properly herself such as washing her own hair. Angie hated such times since it meant sitting in the bath, with its tepid water having done its job of getting herself clean, and then awaiting her mother's application of shampoo and the rough lathering that Angie did not like. She was thankful, however, that the process was over with, in seconds, and her mother was soon done. Thankful, too, that the rough lathering of shampoo, dripping over her tightly shut eyes, could mask her tears since it was the one time she was able to cry and not be detected. She had learned a long time ago that tears provoked slaps and having her hair washed was one time when her mask of resilience could slip back to being a normal five-year-old and, besides, the tears helped to wash away the stinging shampoo from her eyes.

"Right, your hair. Now, get the comb. I'm watching. You know what to do."

Angie made her way over to the dressing table and picked up the comb. Yes, of course she knew what to do. She always combed her own hair. It was only short. She had often wished that she could have long hair just like the pretty dolls her mother gave her and maybe, just maybe then her mother would not think her ugly. Sadly, she recalled once mentioning this to her mother, trying to tell her that she wanted hair like her favourite dolls and then crying when her mother simply laughed, got scissors and hacked off the dolls' hair. All her dolls. All her pretty dolls.

"Right, nearly done. Get your blazer. On the bed. Hurry up."

Angie only saw a jacket on the bed. A dark green jacket and, for a moment, just stared at it. She had never heard of a blazer before but, before panic set in to grip her once more, her mother's blunt direction halted further trepidation.

"Well? What are you waiting for? Put it on."

Angie did as she was told and soon she was ready.

"Fine. Just one last thing. Wait there and I'll go and get it."

Angie did as she was told, not daring to move an inch and, within seconds, her mother was back carrying a bag with a long strap.

"Right. Come here. Just need to adjust the strap for your shoulder. This is your satchel. Inside I've put a pencil case with pens, pencils and colours should you need to use them today."

Angie's confusion started once more to escalate and she tried her very best not to let tears escape since all she wanted to do was cry. Where was it she was going and why would she need to use pens and pencils and colours?

"Well, there you are. Now, what do you say? Well, what do you say?"

Angie knew exactly what she had to say and, without thinking, blurted out her usual mispronunciation of thank you.

"Fank you."

"What was that?"

"F...F... Fank you, mummy."

"There we go again!" her mother exclaimed. "What have I told you before? It's not f… fank you, it's thank you. Th… th…. Put your tongue between your teeth and pronounce it properly!"

Before she knew what was happening, her mother's face was close up to her own staring aggressively, her tongue between her teeth as if pulling a funny face. There was nothing funny about this moment, though, and Angie could taste the fear in her little mouth. The fear was tangible making her want to gag.

"Go on! Tongue between your teeth! Tongue between your teeth!"

Angie, trying hard to compose herself and swallowing back the fear, did as she was told.

"Th...th...thank you," she mumbled.

"What was that? Didn't quite hear you. Say it again. Again, again, again!"

"Thank you, thank you, thank you," Angie remonstrated before her mother could bark at her again. Tongue between teeth, tongue between teeth, tongue between teeth.

"Right. That's better. Time to go."

Where? Angie wondered, trying hard not to voice her curiosity as she followed her mother down the stairs. Her tongue, still between her teeth, now acted as a much needed support, as she bit down on it, stemming the tears that threatened to flow. So many tears, an emotional release too often denied her.

"Right, first day at school and, like I've told you so many times before, children should be seen and not heard. Just remember that. So, you don't need to speak to anyone. Just listen and learn. Listen and learn and nod or shake your head when you have to. Well, you're bloody good at doing that. Or, say yes or no and don't forget to say please when needed and thank you and remember tongue between teeth for that. Okay? Well, are you okay with all of that?"

Angie nodded, fear travelling through her veins but not sketching its might on her face. She knew better than to show any sign of weakness in front of her mother. Yes, at five years old she had been very quick to learn some of the things that triggered her mother. Her mother had many triggers and fear and tears were just a couple of them. A frightened, little girl, crying was never tolerated and so now instead she was screaming inside. School? What and where was school? Her mother had never mentioned it before and Angie was all dressed and ready to go to this place that had a uniform and dark green knickers to match.

CHAPTER 15

'Kind words can be short and easy to speak but their echoes are truly endless.'

Mother Teresa, 1910-1997

June 1960 – First Day

"No time for breakfast, so, just eat this while you're in the car. You'll be getting lunch at school so you'll have to wait till then for something more. Now, mind you don't make a mess with it. Do you hear me? Well?"

Angie nodded as her mother handed over the Cadbury's Flake bar. Melting sweetness that Angie would, at any other time, have welcomed to ease the griping pangs of hunger in her empty stomach; pangs of hunger that often plagued her. Now it was different. Having to eat this chocolate bar in the car without making a mess needed very careful handling. Crumbly, flaky chocolate had a mind of its own and, already fearful and anxious about where her mother was taking her, the chocolate just added to further anxiety. She felt sick and all she wanted to do was get out of the car and run and hide where she could never be found ever again. At least then she could eat the chocolate. She could satisfy the hunger in her belly, letting the flaky crumbs fall and scatter freely onto the wrapper, with the inevitable escapees landing at leisure wherever they chose to, and no need for her to worry at all.

"Are you daydreaming again? Eat your chocolate or, then again, don't eat it. See if I care. If you don't want it then hand it back!"

Angie handed it back.

"You ungrateful little good for nothing. Well, really!"

Angie would rather have starved than be on the receiving end of her mother's displeasure and wrath should a crumb of flaky chocolate escape and land on the car's light coloured upholstery.

The journey itself to school was a blur. Angie did not register her surroundings as they drove along the road. All she knew was that the school must not have been far from home since, very soon, her mother had turned the car off the main road.

Angie had no conception of what life was really like beyond the confines of home and her fear and apprehension grew as the car approached its destination joining a steady stream of other cars. Her mother never took her anywhere except when she had to. Such times were infrequent and usually meant going to a place to see a man that her mother would call 'doctor' and that 'daddy' was one of these as well. At such times she recalled her mother telling her that she had to be good, or else! She recalled sitting on her mother's knee and the cruel, surreptitious grasp-like hugs warning Angie not to squirm or cry. So very young and yet, already, she knew what was not allowed. All she wanted to do was squirm, scream and cry. Her suppressed tears were like a stranglehold round her neck and, when she got home, she would run up the stairs to her bedroom and scream and cry private tears into her pillow until spent.

The cars moved slowly, one behind the other, along a grandiose driveway edged by an archway of trees, and finally sweeping into a wide circle in front of a huge, magnificent building, the likes of which Angie had never seen before. To a little five-year-old girl, as she got out of the car and craned her neck upwards towards the sky, the building, its monumental size and more windows than a casual glance could possibly count, appeared quite intimidating. She tried her best to ignore the milling around of lots of other children dressed in dark green blazers and parents saying their goodbyes, adjusting ties and giving hugs and kisses. Ever since Angie could remember there was always a bizarre hope within her, irrepressible as a bud in spring, that her mother would one day hug her and not call her names and not make her feel so frightened and threatened all the time. She hoped all that had gone on before had just been a mistake, a terrible mistake and that her story held at its heart the potential for a happy ending. She thought now that if today she was really, really good then she would make her mother proud and her mother would be nice and, as her mother grabbed her by the hand and led her into the building, Angie clung on to this small whisper of a chance that she could make her mother happy.

She had never been with lots of other people before. She had never had friends to play with or be with and, the cacophony of sounds and voices as they entered the building, little by little, bit by bit, started to attack the resolve Angie had, only seconds before, made and somehow, somehow she knew that the 'happy ending' she longed for would not happen, at least not today.

"Now, this is your classroom. I shall pick you up later. Remember to be good." Her mother bent down and whispered this into Angie's ear, her tone not gentle but, as usual, stern. Angie was left on her own as other boys and girls found places to sit behind little wooden tables. The tables had lids since some were already being opened and then quickly closed again. Just a few of the boys and girls, though, like Angie, looked lost. Some of them were quietly crying but, on the whole, there was giggling and chatting and a general air of energy and excitement.

Angie's confusion tormented her even more making her head spin. Her mother always told her that children should be seen and not heard yet, in this room made of 'class', the noise was quite deafening. Angie thought that maybe their mothers had not yet instructed them on this rule, a rule that she would never dare break. She looked behind her fully expecting her mother to be spying to see if she joined in and made noise. Her mother was nowhere to be seen. These noisy children obviously knew each other. Friendships had already been formed and Angie was to learn, much later, that they had attended the school before in what was known as the nursery class. Angie had never been to the nursery class and did not know anyone or what to do. She stood still, frozen to the spot where she had been left, desperately wanting to stop the tumultuous feelings that were raging inside her.

"Hello. Angie isn't it?"

Angie's rising panic was suddenly quelled when she felt a tap on her back and her hand was taken and gently squeezed. Angie looked up and saw eyes filled with a kindness, a kindness so genuine, as big as the sea. This lady's eyes were like Judita's and Angie was happy to be led.

"Right, Angie. You sit here. This is your desk. Okay?" Angie nodded and sat down. Focusing her attention on this kind lady was all she needed to do to calm her inner turmoil as she watched further gentleness now being extended to those boys and girls that looked lost and some still crying. The kind lady showed each of them to their places.

"Right, children. Everyone settle down. I shall count to three and, on the count of three, I want absolute silence. One...two..."

There was no need for the third count since silence, complete silence settled over everyone bringing with it a calmness that continued to take away the jagged edges of disquiet that Angie had been feeling.

"Wonderful. Thank you, class. Good morning. Now, my name is Mrs. Carter. I will be your teacher this year and..."

Angie just stared and did not hear any more. What she had suddenly discovered, though, was that all these boys and girls, including herself, were called 'class'. Everything about Mrs. Carter was beautiful and pretty. She wore a bright red lipstick that contrasted with the glow of her pale skin. When she smiled Angie wanted to smile too, even if it was just on the inside.

"Fine. Now, what I would like you all to do is to introduce yourselves, one by one. We shall go round the class and all you need to do is to say, 'Hello or good morning. My name is...' Okay?"

Angie's disquiet returned, burning a fire inside her and she suddenly needed the toilet. The very idea of having to stand up and speak in front of others made her insides feel strange. She did not know proper words or how to form them even though Mrs. Carter had just given them their words. She needed to leave the room and go to the toilet but something told her that you did not just get up and leave. That would be wrong. She would need to be excused but, in front of all these bodies, she had no idea what to say or how to pronounce the words.

As the class started their introductions, some nervously so, others with heads held high and with a degree of confidence that Angie could not quite figure. Angie felt she could not interrupt and, before she knew it, the damage had been done. She had dirtied her knickers. Like pee pee but from her bottom, the smell of the brown liquid inside her knickers rushed at everyone like a blast of heat when an oven door is opened. Her shame and embarrassment was absolute as she heard someone shout out loud, "Ooh, Miss, someone's pooped!" and others expressing their disgust with exclamations of, "Pooooh!" This time there was no holding back the tears. This time, shame and humiliation made Angie sob as her beautiful teacher, wearing the bright red lipstick, took her, once again, gently by the hand and now led her out of the room.

"Everything is going to be just fine, Angie. No need to cry. Little accidents happen all the time. Mrs. Henshaw, our really nice school nurse, will see to you and you'll be right in a jiffy. Okay?"

Angie, head bowed in shame, nodded without looking up.

"Good girl."

Angie could not comprehend her teacher's kind words when she knew exactly what her mother's words would have been. Her mother would not have said she was a good girl. The repercussions of what had occurred would mean having to be on the receiving end of her mother's fury when she found out but, for now, she would allow herself the comfort of kind words and actions.

Just like her teacher, the school nurse was sympathetic and gentle and Angie found herself muttering, over and over, "Sowwy, sowwy, sowwy…"

"No need for you to be sorry, Angie. No need at all. No harm done. Now, let's get you all cleaned up and then some fresh knickers and you'll be as right as rain. Okay?"

Angie nodded and allowed herself to be attended to in the most private of parts, all smelly and dirty, by this very, very kind lady. Her soiled, dark green uniform knickers were put into a little plastic bag and, as soon as Angie was all clean again, the nurse handed her another pair. Dark green uniform knickers, fresh and new.

"There you are. That's better, now, isn't it? We can get these knickers washed for you and we'll be able to give them to mummy later when she comes to pick you up. Okay?"

Angie nodded slowly, knowing it would not be okay when her mother found out and the thought of what her mother might say or do made her sickening fear and panic return. She was so young and puzzled. So much understanding and sympathy, the complete opposites of what she knew to expect from her mother, made her mind stay in turmoil and, because of this, she was secretive and guarded. She did not want her mother to find out and, not being able to vocalise this desperate want, just added to her isolation and sadness. Slow desolate tears started to run from her unblinking eyes and she tried so hard to stem their flow.

"Hey, now, now, there's no need to cry. Listen, I'll tell you what, I'll go and make you a cup of hot, sweet tea and a slice of toast since it's obvious your tummy has been a little upset. Probably all the excitement about starting school. Now, would you like me to do that for you?"

More confusion. Excitement? No! Upset tummy? Her tummy was often upset. Tea and toast? Yes, she would love tea and toast. She could not remember when she had last had anything to eat. She looked up at this lovely lady and, tongue between teeth, she uttered slowly and carefully, "Thank you, thank you. Yes, please."

Not long after and before returning to the classroom, Mrs. Henshaw showed Angie where the girls' toilets were. She told her that the next time she wanted to go to the toilet she only needed to ask permission and there was no need for her to be afraid. If only it was as simple as that, Angie thought to herself. She did not want to have to face the girls and boys in the classroom but knew she would have to. She would need to be brave and pretend that she was on her own and not surrounded by all the other bodies dressed in dark green and grey just as she was. Yes, she needed to be brave.

Taking her gently by the hand Mrs. Henshaw led Angie back into the classroom and to her seat. Angie noticed that a few windows were now open and, remembering to be brave, she tried her best to avoid the sniggers and nudges circulating round some of the other boys and girls as she sat down. Like a chill finding its way to the very core of her being, fear and anxiety started to snarl at Angie, wanting her to cower and cry and allow the glares and stares to suffocate her. Angie took a deep breath. Her bravery would give her strength and, as a furnace, its flames far stronger than any chill, Angie was able to hold her head up high. She looked at her teacher, holding on to her every word. Her beautiful, kind teacher whose calm, soothing tone of voice transported Angie into a dimension of learning and her education began

Mrs. Carter motioned for Angie to open the exercise book already on the desk, pick up the pencil already there too and copy the letters that were being written on the blackboard. She carefully pointed out to write the bigger one of each pair of letters, top to bottom of the lines on the page, and the smaller of the two letters from the fainter line in the middle and down. The blackboard was huge and stood proudly at the front of the classroom. One side of it had lines just like the ones in the exercise books. Two horizontal equally spaced lines and a fainter line in between. Mrs Carter pointed out that if the smaller letter had a 'leg' then this 'leg' was also to be written from top to bottom of the lines with the middle part of the letter in its rightfully placed position from the central line and down. Apart from a few of the other smaller letters needing further additional guidance, Angie did not find the process complicated at all. She listened intently and followed instructions. The class was told that these letters made up the alphabet and, even though some of them might already know a few of their letters, it was very important that they were formed and written down correctly and neatly and in order. Angie did not know her alphabet and, not a stranger to pencils, using colouring ones for all her drawing books at home, she picked up the one that had been left for her on the desk and, with great care and precision, she wrote down the letters across the page: Aa… Bb… Cc… Dd… and so on. These letters were the floodgates to reading and writing that Angie would very soon excel in and, when her beautiful teacher walked round the class, looking at the exercise books and smiling at Angie's endeavours, Angie felt her heart would burst.

"Well done, Angie. Very neat and clear. Good girl."

Proud and beaming, Angie felt she could take on the world and face any further nudges and giggles and pinching of noses that she suspected would not just disappear. Well, not yet anyway.

Lunchtime led to feelings of unease returning when Angie found herself seated at a table in a huge room with other boys and girls from her class. Her beautiful teacher had shown her where she would be sitting from now on, at lunchtimes, and who with, and with a light tap of reassurance on Angie's back that all would be well, she left her there.

All was not well. Far from it. The other boys and girls nearest to her tried to shift themselves away. They isolated her and every nudge and snigger and affected pinching of noses; every underhand, whispered, "Ooh, pooey knickers, pooey knickers!" was like a cruel bite feeding her loneliness and shame. She had been brave before and she wanted to be brave now. She wanted to rekindle the flames that had burned like a furnace earlier giving her the strength to cope when Mrs. Henshaw had taken her back to the classroom. Angie had focused then on her teacher's mellifluous, soothing tones as she specified clearly how to write down neatly and precisely the letters of the alphabet. Angie wanted so much to be back in the classroom with her teacher but, once again, knew she could not just get up and go. If she did, she knew she would draw even more unwanted attention and even more nudges and sniggers and cruel bites that would make her want to cry.

Angie knew she would need to try and focus her mind elsewhere and away from the boys and girls. She looked around the room and, for the first time, noticed its grandeur. The tables were old and made of dark polished wood. The windows, of which there were many, were high up and large and shaped like arched doorways. Angie wondered about the birds that might be flying past and wished she could be one of them at that moment and have the freedom to look in and then fly away. Rectangles of sunlight, like some flamboyant guest not waiting for an invitation, streamed in illuminating the specks of dust swirling in the air.

The rich aroma of food distracted her next and she wondered why she had not noticed it before. She noticed it now. A powerful distraction from the jibes which, for the moment, seemed to have settled. Angie observed older boys and girls helping ladies wearing white uniforms to hand out plates of food to each of the tables. One of the older girls handed over a plate and rested it in front of Angie. Angie looked down at the kind offering, drawn and hypnotised by the meat, gravy, potatoes and vegetables tantalising her taste buds and making her mouth water. A veritable feast. The others at her table had already started to eat their food, the clinking of knives and forks on plates a clear indication, and Angie followed suit.

It did not take long before the older boys and girls came round once more, this time with bowls for each of the young diners. Dessert bowls containing colourful sprinkles, tauntingly scattered upon a creamy mound of ice cream, and Angie almost neglected to pick up her spoon as she eagerly reached for the creamy, melting, sprinkly sweetness. The revulsion Angie had felt from those around her no longer had any impact; such negativity was superseded by lovely food, a staple so inconsistently afforded to Angie in her life and she relished and savoured every nourishing mouthful.

After lunch Angie's class was taken outside to a vast expanse of ground where, as soon as the boys and girls stepped on to it, triggers of complete abandonment reigned. Whoops of delight, shouts and screams, running, chasing, laughter, all loud, shrill and deafening made Angie lean close up against the wall of the building hoping that it would suck her into its very foundations so that she could disappear. She had never experienced playtime with others before and she did not like it. It made her nervous. She wanted to get away and it did not take her long to find a solution. She knew where to go and, without any of the ladies, that now seemed to be in charge, noticing, Angie made her way back inside the building.

Sitting on the cold, hard stone floor, her back resting against the cubicle door, Angie did not notice the numbing chill gradually penetrating through the material of her grey skirt. She had done her best, however, to make sure her bottom was resting on her skirt as she had sat down. Hugging her bended knees and resting her head on them, the noises from outside were now just faint echoes and, as she looked around at the sterile solitude of the toilet cubicle, she felt safe. The eerie quiet of the toilets was broken only by the sound of water dripping, its noise magnified as if in an enclosed space. Though the timing of each drop was fairly erratic, the rate neither increased nor decreased and Angie found it soothing. She let her mind drift away and thought about the shape and order of the letters that her beautiful teacher had shown the class earlier. She tried to remember the bigger letters first followed by their smaller counterparts and then writing them down again in her head. Her mind was thirsty for more knowledge and more learning and she looked forward to listening to her beautiful teacher's words as she explained and showed the class other things. Already, at five years old, Angie was starting to construct a refuge from all the things that threatened to make her nervous and anxious in this place called school. She was going to lose herself in what she was being shown and told in her class by the only person that mattered. No-one else in the class would exist. Her beautiful, kind teacher would be her salvation and Angie felt better.

"Hello! Anyone still in here? Hello! The bell will be going shortly."

Angie's calming thoughts of resilience were interrupted by a voice of authority and she sprang up onto her feet. Slowly opening the cubicle door, she wondered who this voice belonged to and where the bell would be going to?

"Oh, hello there, young lady. Now, are you all done?"

Angie nodded.

"Okay then. Wash your hands. It's time to go and line up with the rest of your class outside before the bell goes."

Angie's curiosity was aroused even further. She knew what a bell was. There was one on the front door at home but where might one go to and how? As she was taken back outside a loud, chaotic clanging suddenly added to the vibrant noises of the boys and girls still playing and running around. Angie saw one of the ladies, in charge, holding and swinging something dome-shaped in her hand. With each swing the noises in the yard were quietened by a powerful reverberated clanging summoning the end of play.

"There you are. That's the bell. Told you it would go. Now, line up with your class over there."

The lady pointed to the line of dark green and grey and Angie made her way to the very back of it establishing in her mind, as she did so, that a bell 'going' meant a bell clanging and that there must be different types of bells. Despite its loud clamour, Angie was fascinated by this sort of bell and would love to have been its bearer.

Angie's resolve to be strong in the classroom remained steadfast as she swathed herself in a wonderland of discovery listening to her beautiful teacher's instructions and trying her very best to follow them.

On each desk a piece of paper, with some of the letters from the alphabet written down on it, had been placed. The class was told that these letters spelled out their names and that the first letter of the name must always be the bigger of the letter pairs. Angie learned that these bigger letters were called capital letters. She carefully located each of the letters in her name from the alphabet letters she had written down earlier in her exercise book and then, as neatly as she could, started to write down her name over and over again. The piece of paper, that had been left on the desk, acted as a guide. It was really just like copying a drawing and Angie was fascinated.

The class was told that they were writing down their first name only and that this name was known as their Christian name. Angie wanted to know why it was called a Christian name and, when they were told that in their next writing lesson they would be copying down their family name, their second name, also termed as their surname, Angie's curiosity was raised to another level. Why Christian name and why surname but she kept quiet and hoped someone else would ask why. No-one ever did and, it was only some years later, when she looked it up in a dictionary, that her curiosity was sated.

Engrossed in the task assigned to her Angie was sad when the class was told to close their books and put their pencils down. Angie felt that she could have carried on forever and ever and ever but did as she was told. She looked at her beautiful teacher whose red lipstick still contrasted with the glow of her pale skin and, this time, Angie's lips broadened into the faintest of smiles. The class was told that soon the bell would be 'going' but, before it did, there was time for a story. Story time. Angie's first experience of anyone ever having read to her before and she never forgot it. 'The Giving Tree' set Angie's imagination in a whirl as she lived each moment of her beautiful teacher's telling of this poignant, moving tale.

The clamorous clanging of the bell signalling the end of the school day acted as a rude awakening since Angie knew that she would soon have to face the inevitable outcome of her 'little accident'. Dread, fear and trepidation were now the victors and this time, despite taking deep breaths, their presence started to snarl at Angie making her feel suffocated.

All the way home her mother never looked at her. She did not say a word. Not a single word, intensifying Angie's fear even more. She wanted so much to loosen the tie around her neck and try to catch her breath. The anticipated beating, slaps and kicks; the horrid, cruel words, however, never came. Instead, once inside the house, what happened was far worse. Her mother never spoke. Not a single slur, not a single smear. Nothing. As she stood in the hallway, looking up at her mother and into her eyes, the unmoving blue pools of ice hit Angie harder than any sharp, stinging, painful slap or kick. With one of her perfectly manicured fingers her mother motioned Angie up the stairs and to her room. Making her way there the chill of her mother's voice, as she laid down clear instructions, made Angie wince and tremble.

"Take off your uniform. Fold it neatly. Leave it on your chair. Bathroom. Wash. A good wash all over. Between your legs and your bottom. Your dirty, filthy bottom. Wash it! Wash it! Wash it! Then, get into your bed and don't move! Do not come out!"

Angie did exactly as she was told and thankful that, at least, she had had something to eat at school. A veritable feast. Meat, gravy, vegetables and potatoes followed by a creamy mound of ice cream. Vanilla ice cream with colourful sprinkles tauntingly scattered over the top. Yes, a veritable feast.

CHAPTER 16

'He who opens a school door closes a prison.'

Victor Hugo, 1802-1885

1960 - 1965

School very soon became Angie's safe haven, an escape from the storms she tried so hard to weather on a daily basis at home. At five years old it was very difficult to comprehend her mother's unpredictable behaviour and Angie found herself despising and not liking her mother at all for the way she made her feel. She instilled in her a fear that spoke in toxic, cackling tones. The fear would tell her legs to go weak, it would tell her stomach to lurch and it would tell her very young heart to ache. The fear was masterful and Angie hated herself for finding her mother so horrid. Her feelings made her feel shame and guilt. The guilt at despising her mother was very difficult for Angie. She was still too young to understand her emotions fully and felt that she must have just been a bad girl, a very bad girl indeed…

The morning after her 'little accident' Angie was roused early from sleep by noises coming from the bathroom. Strange noises. Rubbing her eyes, Angie got out of bed and made her way to the bathroom. Her mother was the one making these noises, kneeling on the floor with her head bent over the toilet as she heaved and heaved and was being sick. All Angie could do was stand there and watch until the retching stopped and a pungent, sour smell hit her nostrils. Pale and shivering and smelly, her mother leant back against the bathroom wall. Apart from her mother not wearing any shoes, Angie noticed that her clothes were the ones she had worn the previous day when she had brought Angie home from school. It was not like her mother to wear the same clothes on consecutive days. She assumed that her mother must have really liked this outfit although, at present, it was crumpled and creased and stained. She would probably want to change it now before taking Angie to school.

As her mother lay limp and helpless with her eyes closed and her chest heaving and gasping for each new breath, Angie was frightened. She did not know what to do.

"Mummy? Mummy? Mummy?" she found herself repeating. It was all she knew to say to vocalise her concern and fear.

"Water. Water. Get me some water!" her mother mumbled, moving her head from side to side against the tiles of the wall.

Angie quickly did as she was told. She brought out her little stool from the side of the sink so that she could reach the cabinet above it. She picked up the white plastic beaker that she knew was in there and filled it with cold water. Being very careful not to spill any of the water, Angie stepped down off her stool and knelt by her mother.

"Mummy? Mummy? Water."

With a trembling, shaking hand her mother took the beaker and started to sip slowly from it. All the while Angie knelt by her, her brain desperately scrambling to make some sense of it all. She had never before seen her mother like this. She did not like it.

"Okay. Now, help me back to my room."

Leaving the empty beaker on the floor, her mother slowly got to her feet using the tiled wall as a support. Not really knowing how to help, Angie could only stand and walk by her mother's side. Unsteadily, her mother made her way back to the bedroom, one hand on the wall and the other reaching out for Angie to hold. Angie held on to its shaking, quivering grip.

"Now, just let me lie down and have a few minutes before I get ready to take you to that bloody school. Go and get yourself washed and then put your uniform on. You know what to do and make sure to clean up any mess in the bathroom. Do you hear me?"

Silence.

"Well?"

"Yes, mummy."

"Go on, then."

As Angie left the room her mother, with eyes once again closed, turned over onto her side. Angie noticed a damp patch on her mother's skirt and discovered later, when cleaning the mess in the bathroom, that there was a wet pool on the linoleum where her mother had been sitting. Her mother must have had an accident too; hers was not runny poo poo but wee. Her mother had wet her knickers; the dirty, wet, smelly ones that Angie had found by the side of the toilet.

It was the first time Angie had ever had to clean up her mother's dirt and mess and it would not be the last. In a panic she wet the flannel and wiped it over the wee wee puddle on the lino. It was strong and unpleasant and she soon realised that the wet flannel would not be enough to clean up properly. She needed something that would smell nice. She opened the big cupboard in the bathroom where she had seen Judita bring out all her cleaning essentials when she was doing her chores in there. She opened a plastic bottle that Judita often used and put her nose over it. Whatever it was, smelled very pleasant. Trying hard not to pour too much from the bottle, that was nearly full to the top and quite heavy, she tilted it over the floor but the liquid seemed to have a mind of its own and flowed freely from the nozzle leaving a big puddle. As she got towels to wipe over it, the floor started to feel sticky. Not what she wanted to happen. She got one of the cloths from the cupboard and wet it. Eventually, after wiping over and over the stickiness and using a couple of towels to dry her attempt at ridding the mess her mother had left, Angie could do no more. Her motivation to avoid the wrath of her mother meant she had done her very best and now she needed to get herself ready for school just as she had been instructed.

As the years progressed and her mother's drinking became more frequent and heavier, Angie would find herself cleaning up far worse than wee and sick. In an attempt to keep her mother's magazine cover replica of relaxation and affluence pristine, Angie soon learned what to do so as not to be on the receiving end of her mother's displeasure, once sober, when Angie would be blamed for any mess remotely still in evidence.

Clean and clean and clean. Over and over. Remove any sick or poo from carpet or walls with toilet paper. Flush away the horrid, stinky mess. Some soapy, cold water and soak and rub away the horrid, stinky, stain. Over and over. Blot dry. Job done. Yes, Angie, from such a young age, soon became quite the expert…

Apart from the buttons, Angie's uniform was not a problem. Even the tie over her head and the shirt collar raised up and then placed over it, thankfully proved straightforward. It was just the buttons, which were soon mastered when Angie remembered to start from the bottom button up. She waited for her mother downstairs in the kitchen and had only dared to get herself a glass of water to drink. So much had happened since first waking up that Angie did not feel hungry and, if yesterday was anything to go by, she would be getting something to eat at school. She knew better than to sneak something to eat for herself from the kitchen. Her mother would not be pleased and, considering how poorly her mother had been earlier, Angie did not want to risk any further upset. She had already heard her mother in the bathroom and the toing and froing from the bedroom and wondered how much longer her mother was going to be. With her satchel strap still on her shoulder Angie was ready to leave. Despite the other boys and girls who might still probably giggle and pinch their noses when they saw her, Angie wanted to go to school and see her beautiful teacher who made her feel settled and safe and transported her mind to calmer waters and a vast, endless sea of learning. She tried to remember the letters in her name and still thought about the word 'Kistian'. 'Kistian name'. Why? Why, 'Kistian'? What did it mean?

"Are you dreaming again? No time to stand there dawdling. We're going to be late. Well, come on. Get a move on!"

Stirred out of her thoughts by her mother's sharp tone, Angie jumped and quickly moved out of the way as her mother nudged her aside and went to get something from one of the cupboards.

"Wait!"

Angie froze. What had she done? Had she done something wrong already?

"Here. Eat this. We do not want a repetition of yesterday. Do you hear me? Do you understand? Well?"

Her mother handed her a biscuit and, as she looked up, Angie could not quite believe how different her mother now looked. No longer dishevelled and dirty her mother was dressed in a trouser suit of cream with blue stripes and make up on her face. Unlike her beautiful teacher's vibrant red lipstick her mother's was the usual insipid beige colour that blended into a dull face that Angie never saw smile.

"Well, are you going to take it? Hurry up. Eat it now in here so that you won't be dropping any crumbs in the car."

Thankful for that, Angie took the biscuit and bit into its crumbly sweet taste, however, still trying to catch any loose miscreants just in case. She need not have worried since her mother was already leaving the house and getting into the car. Angie quickly hurried after her, standing on tiptoe to shut the front door.

"Now, I can't be doing this every bloody morning. Having to take you to school. It's not going to work. So, I've had an idea. Yes, an idea. I'm going to have a word with Bob to arrange for him to take you to school in the mornings. I'm sure he won't mind coming to the house on his days off as well as when he comes to do the garden. He'll appreciate the extra money. I'll see him today. Might even get him to pick you up after school on Tuesdays and Thursdays and Fridays when he's already here. Save me having to do it. Obviously not today. I'll have to sort it all first. Yes, I think it's a very good idea. What do you think?"

Angie had been trying very hard to keep up with what her mother was saying but was soon lost. She could not quite fully comprehend the full extent of what was being suggested.

"Well?" her mother asked

Silence.

"Well? What do you think? Have you actually been listening to me?"

Somewhat perplexed, Angie nodded slowly.

"Well, is that a 'yes'?" her mother demanded, taking her eyes off the road for a minute.

Angie could feel the tension starting to build within the confines of the car and she wanted to get out.

"A nod. Always a bloody nod. Nod, nod, bloody nod. Answer me properly. What do you think?"

Angie's mind was in its usual turmoil. She had forgotten what she was meant to be thinking about but then, thankfully, was prompted by her mother.

"Well, do you think it's a good idea?"

"Yes, yes, mummy. Yes, mummy," Angie mumbled, still somewhat unsure as to what the idea actually meant.

"Yes, mummy, what?"

"F... f… thank you, mummy," tongue between teeth, "th… thank you, mummy."

"Right. That's that, then."

And, so it was. Bob became Angie's personal driver and she could not have been happier. She had only ever waved to Bob through the window whenever he was tending to the garden and he always waved back or gave her a thumbs up. Like Judita, he always had a smile for her. She would watch him working, often finding herself wanting to escape the heavy atmosphere ever present inside the house when her mother was there. She wanted to run around and around the wide lawn that he tended with such care and precision. She never did. It was not allowed. Her mother would not allow it. It would mean muddying her clothes if she fell down and that would never do.

Angie had never heard Bob speak before. He was only ever a figure that waved and smiled and did not seem to mind Angie watching him through her bedroom window. Despite feeling nervous the very first time he arrived to drive her to school, she was thankful that, at least, she would not have to experience her mother's venom that could bite at whim as Angie sat next to her in the car.

Angie was waiting at the door. Her mother had left her there to wait alone. Bob was using her father's car, the one that was kept in the garage for whenever he came home, which did not seem to be often. Her mother had arranged it since she did not want Angie turning up at school in, 'a scruffy old van'. Angie had been a little excited, though, about going inside 'a scruffy old van'. It was white with letters from the alphabet written on the sides.

"Good morning, young lady. Your carriage awaits," were the first words she ever heard Bob say and, straightaway, any jitters she may have had were dispelled. She did not know what a carriage was but assumed it was her father's car and she liked the name. She tried to pronounce the word in her head but, for now, it proved difficult. She would need to practise.

The back door of the 'carriage' was opened for her and Angie climbed inside. Bob took her satchel and held it for her as she did so. Once seated inside, with her satchel resting on her knees, Angie felt very small. Unlike the compact interior of her mother's car, this car was grand and she found herself wanting to slide her bottom around the black, smooth, shiny seat that spread across its vast width, but did not. Instead, she remained still and straight-backed like a good little girl.

Right from the start Angie's journeys to and from school with Bob became an education in themselves. His voice had a deep, husky drawl which would often calm any swirling pain in her head that would still be there from what her mother might have said, or made her do, or what had been left for her to do. In Bob's presence there was a calmness that steadily eased her pain bringing some peace and balance. From Bob she learned all about nature, a subject very dear to him. She learned the names of flowers and herbs and different trees and how magical a garden can be. He even told her that some plants and flowers bloom at night. A moon garden and a time when the fairies would come out to play. He told her that the fairies were beautiful and delicate and, with their fluttery, feathery wings would dance and fly and play in the moonlight when the world was asleep. In the daytime they would rest under the oak and ash trees in the garden all safe and sound and, if she were to take a peep under the branches, making sure to avoid the sharp thorns, she might just catch a glimpse of one! Angie's imagination was blessed with Bob's knowledge and words and sometimes, whenever she was feeling sad and frightened, she imagined shrinking to fairy size and hiding and sleeping under the branches of the oak tree, in the far corner of the garden, safe from her mother and protected by fairy magic.

Any silences in the car were never awkward. They were just comfortable, surrounding her and smoothing out the ever present roughness of her life at home.

Mrs. Carter was the best classroom teacher and she was Angie's support. A mainstay in a life that was filled with so much disquiet. Her teacher's beautiful smile, the red lipstick always so carefully applied, made a lasting impression on Angie and she hoped that one day, when she was older, she would wear red on her lips and be beautiful too.

Her teacher's gentle yet authoritative manner meant that the class got its work done and no-one was made to feel uncomfortable. In the classroom the boys and girls were taught to read and write and be creative as they drew and painted pictures and made things with plasticine. The atmosphere was fun and light. Mrs. Carter made it so. Outside the classroom, though, the boys and girls could still be cruel with their taunting laughter and smirks, never letting Angie forget about her 'little accident'.

Apart from lunchtime, where she savoured every mouthful of food on her plate and not quite believing how some of the boys and girls at her table left so much of theirs, Angie's first few days at school, outside the classroom, meant that she would once more seek solace and refuge in the girls' toilets, away from the noise and the threat of insults being thrown like punches and hurting her. After her very first day she knew to wait for the clang, clang, clang of the bell that summoned the end of play but, before any clanging, one of the ladies in charge would always find her there and make sure she lined up with the rest of her class to go back inside and to the relative peace and quiet of the classroom where she wanted to be.

Angie's place of escape was soon found out, however, when, one day, Mrs. Carter found her hiding away and, without any questions being asked, she took her by the hand and led her back to the classroom. Empty of bodies, and only the hush of lunchtime, the classroom felt surreal. Her beautiful teacher looked down at Angie and smiled.

"Angie, in future, once you've had your lunch, would you prefer to spend the rest of the time here? You can look after the reading books in the library corner and tidy them up. You can also look through them. It will help your reading. You can tidy up around the classroom as well if you like. The classroom door is always left wide open at lunchtime and the staffroom's only opposite so I can keep bobbing in and out to see that you're okay. How does that sound?"

For the first time in her miserable life Angie felt a measure of what happiness was like. A beam of light to the soul, this resolution felt like a huge weight of despair was lifted from her tiny shoulders and she stood tall and beamed.

"Thank you," she uttered. "Thank you. Thank you. Thank you," she repeated and no longer needed to think about having to put her tongue between her teeth.

Angie's love of reading was born as she tidied all the books in the library corner and arranged them in height order with their spines showing. Some of the books she would stand up so that their designs and front cover illustrations were like magnets for any reader. One of the books was especially enchanting and caught Angie's attention straightaway since it confirmed what Bob had told her about fairies and how magical and precious they were.

At five years old, with the help of the 'Ladybird' series of books that she loved to tidy away on the shelves, she learned to read quickly. All of them the same pocket-size, with their colourful illustrations and captivating stories, they were easy to stand up straight and neatly together in their rows. The Peter and Jane Learning to Read titles became her friends. Even though she found it difficult to relate to Jane helping mummy bake cakes or Peter helping daddy fix the car, she was still happy since they helped her to read. She followed Peter and Jane in their adventures and was taken to wonderful new places so very far removed from her own life.

She loved her job and was proud to be in charge of it. None of the other boys and girls wanted to be her friend anyway and she managed to block them out, building a stone wall around herself so they would not get in and steal her happiness. Those that called her names soon grew bored and, apart from the occasional, 'pooey knickers, pooey knickers', and the pinching of noses, there was nothing. Excluding and blanking only and Angie could not have been any more pleased.

An astute and clever girl, she progressed quickly in her lessons and gained high scores. She felt that failure would mean she was letting her beautiful, kind teacher down and she would never let that happen. Even going up into the next class and beyond, Angie was still allowed to go and tidy the classroom and books for Mrs. Carter. After doing her jobs, she was able to sit and read quietly while the other boys and girls were playing.

Angie made the most of attending school. The compassion and understanding that her beautiful teacher had shown her, from the very start, was a shining light giving her the courage to believe in herself and embrace all learning.

All the teachers were kind and they too made her feel safe. Some were very strict, others not so but Angie did not mind since they knew just how much she wanted to learn and how quick she was to learn. Her brain was like a sponge soaking up every drop of knowledge it could and it was not long before the taunt of 'pooey knickers' was replaced with, 'clever clogs' and even, 'teacher's pet', both of which did not bother Angie at all since she was generally left alone and refused to let any name-calling infiltrate her love of school.

Mrs. Carter would often say, "Angie. You're an absolute gem. Don't know where I would be without you. The classroom is always so tidy and the books are all beautifully arranged and in order."

At such times Angie felt so proud.

Her proudest moment, though, came when, aged nine, she was promoted to school library monitor, the finest of accolades and Angie was fit to burst. She wore her badge with great dignity for all the world to see on her school blazer. She had also been given one to wear on her cardigan. Her mother did not even notice. Her mother could not have cared less.

Her position in the school library meant the world to Angie and introduced her to many different writers and genres. Books were her treasures. Perhaps it was because of the turmoil in her own life that she immersed herself in the immeasurable power of words that gave her emotions a secret home. To have been given her job meant that the teachers held her in high regard and she was grateful to them all. One day, though, shortly after being presented with her badge of office at a school assembly, it was announced that Mrs. Carter would be leaving to have her baby. At the mention of this news Angie's thoughts were suddenly sent into a dizzying spin as she tried to understand and accept what she had heard. Having a baby? Leaving? She knew that mummies had babies. How it happened, she had no idea. She had been a baby once and knew that her mother had not really wanted her when she came. Her mother had once told her that the day Angie had arrived, in December, had been a freezing cold day and for Christmas, instead of a baby, she would have much preferred a handbag. Still, daddy was happy and loved mummy for giving him a little girl who would grow and grow to be beautiful. It had not worked that way, though. Daddy had stayed in the army and her mother had been left on her own to look after a dirty, smelly baby, that kept her from enjoying herself and was so hideous, ugly and vile that daddy chose to stay away.

Angie could not imagine never again seeing Mrs. Carter's beautiful smile and bit down on her lip so as not to cry. Her tears threatened for the rest of the morning until she was able to go and see her.

"Angie, Angie, don't be upset. What better timing. You're now an important school library monitor, a position that I know you will excel in, and there'd be little time for my room, anyway. You are moving on and I couldn't be prouder. It's time for me now to start a family of my own."

She watched, as Mrs. Carter gently stroked her hand round and round the mound on her belly that Angie had not noticed until that moment.

"Is your baby in there?" Angie asked. None of the books Angie had read, as yet, explained where babies actually came from and how they got there.

"Yes, it is. Sleeping soundly at the moment. All quiet and snug yet, at times, it can kick and kick and then I know it's going to be a lively baby."

Angie wanted to ask how it would get out of there but knew it was rude to ask too many questions and so let it remain a mystery for the time being.

"Angie. What you can do for me from now on is continue to do your very best in class and enjoy your position in the library, which I know you will. Angie, you're going to be just fine. Okay?"

Angie looked up at the beautiful red smile beaming down on her. Red lipstick, as ever, meticulously applied, unlike her mother's bland beige, that was often smeared and smudged making her look like a crazy clown, whenever Angie had to clean her up. With eyes now fixed on her teacher's smile, Angie nodded and nodded again and the tears escaped, one after the other, rolling steadily down her pinched and pale cheeks.

Wherever she was in school, thereafter, and whatever it was she was doing, Angie would always try to imagine that Mrs. Carter was a fly on the wall watching her and pleased with all her endeavours. This very thought would drive Angie on even more to excel and she did. She had found a way of coping with a loss that she could not fathom at first and so her imagination became her salvation. In the library she was a great asset and reports were sent home praising all her work and her achievements. Her mother would read them and then just throw them in the waste bin not wanting to clutter the house with pieces of paper.

Angie likened her mother to the wicked stepmother in Cinderella and was still waiting for a fairy godmother to come and rescue her and magic her away. There were times when she would look out through the window at the old oak tree down at the bottom of the garden and wish her fairy godmother would wake up. The fairies, and all that she had read about them, were still firmly fixed in the realms of her make-believe but this was soon to change. No more beautiful, fluttery fairies and no fairy godmother bringing magic. December,1965, as

Angie turned ten years old and her father, Dr. John Arthur Ross, came home to stay, all her make-believe magic would be gone.

CHAPTER 17

'And yet to every bad there is a worse…'

Thomas Hardy, 1840-1928

December 1965 – Homecoming

Birthdays were hardly celebrations. Her mother would often come into Angie's room, anyway, to throw something on the bed, like new clothes or shoes and toys and games to play with. As she started to get older, though, Angie so wanted to choose things for herself. Birthdays were nothing special at all. No fancy wrapping paper or bows, or a card.

Angie's tenth birthday was no exception. Her mother came into her room and threw a box on the bed

"Here. A birthday present. It's a talking doll. You can have conversations with it. Just pull a string and she'll say things back. Might stop all that bloody daydreaming you do! Now, get a move on. Bob will be here shortly to take you to school."

Another doll? Proof enough that her mother did not know her at all. Angie would have loved a book to read instead. Her very own book and not one borrowed from school.

She looked at the box. Quite a big box and, on the front of it, she read the name: Chatty Cathy. This doll was 'chatty'! Intrigued, Angie took the doll out of its box. The doll was cute and had long, blonde wavy hair. It was sturdy and stood up straight on legs that were chubby. There was a ring pull at the back of the doll's neck. She read the instructions on the box and pulled the white plastic ring out slowly, as far as it would go, and then released it. As the cord made its way back into the neck Angie was greeted with the words, "Please take me with you." Intrigued even more, Angie pulled the ring out again and this time Chatty Cathy said, "I love you." Angie was taken aback. It was the first time these words were ever spoken in her presence and she did not know whether to laugh or cry. Words Angie had always wanted her mother to say but her mother never did and now, instead, the words came from something inanimate. Not real. Still, sometimes that was what she now came to think of her mother. Not real, cold, devoid of feelings. No feelings at all. Angie took one last look at the doll and put it back in its box. Chatty Cathy was never brought out again.

Even though it had only been just a few days ago, Angie's birthday was of no consequence at all. She did not feel any different. Ten years old and she might as well have been a doll, like the one she had received for her birthday and then her mother would only have to pull a string and Angie would be allowed to speak. Angie knew, however, that if she were a Chatty Cathy doll, her mother would probably never choose to pull the string and would be happy for her daughter to remain quiet forever.

Fridays meant no more school for a couple of days and Angie hated them. They heralded the weekend when there was no escaping the presence of her mother and the aftermath of too much drinking from the bottles regularly stocked in the drinks' cabinet. All neatly lined up and next to each other. As soon as she was able to read Angie had discovered that her mother's favourite friends were the bottles labelled Vodka. Finding her mother lying on the landing, her usual resting place after a night's drinking, or being sick in the toilet, or having wet herself or pooed, Angie would clean up after her and make sure everywhere was tidy and things put away. In the living room the drinks' cabinet was predominantly the home of Vodka bottles although there were a few other bottles, too. She read the labels: Gin, Whiskey, Brandy and, as she looked at the brown liquids and those that looked just like water except in fancy glass bottles, she wondered why and how they could be so harmful as to often leave her mother in such terrible states and ones that she could hardly remember except to say to Angie, the day after, that she had a dreadful headache and needed to rest.

Weekends seemed to be worse when her mother's drinking would often start early in the day. Weekends meant no food on the table at all and hardly anything in the cupboards. Sometimes, though, when she knew her mother would no doubt be in a slumber on the settee and she could hear her snores coming from the living room, Angie would sneak into the kitchen and salvage whatever she could without her mother finding out. Usually, a stale slice of bread or stale biscuit that would at least ease, for a short time, the rumblings in her stomach.

Weekends meant Angie would make sure that she always brought home more than enough to read and to keep her occupied. As well as any homework that might have been issued, her teachers knew how keen she was in her studies and let her take home as many books as she wanted. They knew she was reliable and so were always assured of their safe return. She liked to read non-fiction too, looking for answers to questions she could never ask her mother or want to bother her teachers about. And so, in the absence of explanations, Angie would develop her own theories, either invented, or as a result of something she had read. Ever since she had seen Mrs Carter gently stroking the mound on her belly, where her baby was, she had been intent on finding out how babies got there and how they came out. The nearest she got to some sort of an explanation was from one of the Golden Treasury of Knowledge volumes where she discovered that hens laid eggs as well as birds and reptiles and that, when the eggs cracked, their babies came out. As for human babies she eventually developed the theory that maybe mummies were able to buy special human baby eggs, which were only very small, much smaller than the ones she had sometimes seen Judita putting in the fridge and which were meant to be cooked and eaten.

Being very careful to swallow the human baby egg whole, without the shell breaking, the egg would then be able to grow and grow inside the warmth of the mummy's belly. After a while the shell would crack and the baby would be able to wriggle about and sleep and kick around, just as Mrs. Carter's baby did. Not long after, when the baby was ready to be born, it would slide out one day when its mummy went to the toilet for a wee wee. At ten years old Angie held onto this theory and just wondered where her mother had got her egg from and whether her daddy had been there at the time. Her mother had already told her that it was her father who had wanted a little girl and that she would have been happier with a handbag when Angie had arrived. All Angie could assume was that her mother must have just chosen the wrong egg and, once swallowed, there was nothing that could be done about it. Eventually, when Angie discovered the truth about babies, she much preferred her own theory.

"Okay, young lady. Here we are. There's been a lot going on today. Your mother's no doubt told you already about your father coming home pretty soon and so she's getting a few jobs done before he does. Anyway, the workmen are still here and so is Judita. Your mother's asked her to stay on so that she can clean up after the jobs have been finished. So, see you Monday. Your carriage will be waiting at its usual time."

Usually, Angie would giggle at Bob's words, which were always the same as he opened the door and helped her out of the car. Today, though, she did not giggle. She just looked up at Bob's gentle face and tried her best to smile so as not to appear rude. Confused and full of questions she looked at the vans outside the house and heard noises coming from within. The front door was already wide open and, after saying thank you and goodbye to Bob, Angie made her way inside.

Her mother had not told her a thing. Her father was coming home. Over the years he had been home before but this was different. Jobs were being done this time and she could not understand why. As soon as Judita saw her she explained everything. Her father was coming home to stay. He was not going back to the army. He was now going to be a doctor near home. New carpets were being fitted and a shower was being installed in the bathroom. Her mother wanted everywhere pristine and fresh and modern. Judita tried to explain that an electric shower in the bathroom was for rich people and that Angie was a lucky girl having such a beautiful home.

How many times had Judita used the word lucky to describe Angie and, once again, Angie wished she could tell her the truth? Being lucky suggested happiness and joy and good things happening. Angie's life at home was so very far removed from anything lucky at all. Lucky meant being able to sleep soundly at night without the worry of her mother invading her room and reminding Angie just how ugly, vile and hideous a little girl she was. Lucky meant being able to sleep soundly at night without having to get up and check on her mother. Lucky meant not having to clean up messes. Lucky meant feeling calm and safe and being able to run outside and play freely and get muddy and laugh and sing and dance and her mother smiling and laughing, too. No. Angie did not feel lucky. Far from it. Still, maybe her father coming home would change that. Her father coming home might make her mother smile and start to like Angie more. Maybe it would. Yes, just maybe it would...

It had not stopped raining all day bringing with it blustery gusts of wind, darkness and gloom and cold. From first being driven to school in the morning, to now being driven home, Angie could not remember a day like it. Despite it being winter this still should have been a bright day, a happy, light day to celebrate the occasion of her father's homecoming. As the rain lashed unmercifully against the car windows, Angie could not help thinking about something she had recently learned in class. The class was being told about the Elizabethans, in one of their history sessions, and how people were very superstitious at that time. The word itself, superstitious, fascinated Angie since, aged 10, she did not understand what it actually meant nor could she pronounce it properly and had to keep saying it over and over in her head until she got it nearly right. Her teacher explained what the word meant and Angie's interest was further engaged. One of the things the Elizabethans believed was that bad weather, really bad weather, was a sign that something untoward, something really terrible and not right, was happening somewhere or had happened or was about to…

"A penny for them."

"Umm. Pardon?"

"A penny for your thoughts, young lady. Honestly, Angie, if I were to have actually given you a penny for every time I've said that to you, you'd be a millionaire right now! Well, I bet you'll be thinking about your father and excited to see him. It's been a long while since he was last home and this time he's here to stay. Yes, bet you can't wait to see him."

Angie giggled. Bob was right. She had been lost once again in her thoughts and had not noticed that the car had pulled up onto the drive. It was still raining and still very windy as Bob opened the back passenger door to help her out.

"Okay, then, young lady. See you Monday morning. Your carriage will await at its usual time."

"Thank you, Bob. See you Monday," Angie replied, as she hurried indoors to meet her father.

Angie did not really know how to feel. Bob used the word excited but she was not quite sure if that was how she was feeling now. Her father had never been a constant in her life. On the few occasions when he had been home, albeit not for long, apart from bringing her new toys to play with and sitting her on his knee and asking her how she was, he mainly spent his time with her mother and she was told that she was to be a good girl and stay in her room. Her mother would tell her that they did not want to be disturbed. Her father had never asked her what she liked or did not like. She expected her mother did not have much to tell him about their daughter since she knew little about what Angie liked or was interested in herself. Chatty Cathy, in its box in the cupboard, was clear testament to this.

Once inside the house the strong, heavy muskiness of her mother's perfume filled the air and Angie hated it more than ever. Her mother had applied far too much of the sickly sweetness and Angie wondered whether it was because her father was home and he liked it. As she removed her shoes in the hallway, she could hear laughter coming from the living room. Her mother's laughter was loud and exaggerated and Angie knew, then, that her mother must have had too much to drink already.

The living room door was wide open but Angie stood fixed in the hallway. She did not know what to do. What was she expected to do? Whenever her mother was in there, Angie was never allowed entry until knocking on the door and then being invited in. She was never allowed to sit on the sumptuous cream leather settee and watch the television or read. This was her mother's space and her mother did not want her in the way. The only time she ever went in there was to help her mother to bed and clean up messes and tidy things away. At such times she still knocked on the door just in case her mother was sober enough to sort herself out. Maybe, now that her father was home, things would be better.

"Hello! Is that my little girl out there?"

Angie's thoughts were interrupted by a deep, throaty voice, "Well, where are you? Aren't you coming to say hello?"

She made her way to the living room. Her father was smoking and, like her mother, he had a glass in his hand, too. He was not as tall as she remembered but he was very broad and he was smiling. As he looked at Angie, he took a further drink from the glass before putting it down and, stubbing out the cigarette in the ashtray, he made his way towards her with arms outstretched.

"Come and give your daddy a big hug, then."

Angie looked at her mother first as if for approval and her mother nodded. Before she could move, she was wrapped in her father's strong embrace. Perhaps too strong. Angie felt smothered as he held her very closely and then nuzzled his face into her neck, kissing her; his smoky breath trapping itself in her hair. She was glad when he stepped back and felt guilty that she had not liked her father's hug.

"My, my, you've grown. You're a real beauty. Yes, indeed. A real beauty."

Angie was stunned. She did not know what to think as her father slowly looked at her up and down. In the silence that followed she felt awkward and uncomfortable and was glad when her mother told her to go into the kitchen and get herself a chocolate bar to eat for later. Her mother and father wanted 'together time'. They had lots of catching up to do and Angie was dismissed, as her father turned his back on her and went to pour himself another drink.

Her father being home meant that, for the first week or so, there was a lot of 'together time' when he and her mother did not want to be disturbed. For much of the

Christmas holiday, except for Christmas Day itself, Angie had little to eat except for chocolate and possibly some stale bread that she managed to sneak from the kitchen when her parents were drinking in the living room, or when they were making strange noises in the bedroom. She would sometimes hear the same strange noises, when they were in the bathroom together, and under the swell of the new shower's rushing stream of water, for what seemed a very long time.

Christmas Day, though, was different. Family time and it was not long before Angie wanted to get back to her room. As a child she knew only too well that she was without power or choice, always having to abide by a change in wind and always praying for a safe harbour.

Angie's safe harbour was school and, after reading the whole series of Enid Blyton's, 'Malory Towers', she wished she too was at boarding school, away from home, and not having to dread evenings and weekends. At home, except for when her mother would sometimes intrude, Angie's harbour was her bedroom and her escape into literature and more learning.

Outside caterers had been brought in to prepare and serve the Christmas dinner with all the trimmings. The Christmas tree had been decorated by professionals, too. Her mother preferred to pay for people to do things for her and, now that Angie's father was home, she said that her time was precious and she refused to waste it on things that she hated doing anyway.

On Christmas Day Angie was given specific instructions to keep out of the way until she was called down to dinner. The table was beautifully laid out and the food was delicious. She savoured every mouth-watering, scrumptious bite, each chew and swallow and made sure to say thank you when one of the ladies served her. Angie noticed, though, that neither her mother nor her father afforded the ladies the same courtesy and generally ignored them. Angie thought her parents rude as they only had time for each other and drank far too much.

After the meal she asked permission to leave the table. Up until that moment she had not spoken a word and now, when she did, it was like time standing still. An eerie sort of silence seemed to fill the room and heighten her senses.

"Angie, Angie, Angie, my little darling," her father finally said, looking at her, bleary eyed and smiling. Angie did not know whether to smile back as, for the first time since starting dinner, he took notice of her.

"Well, let's have a closer look at you in your new dress before we let you go. Stand up, then."

Angie got up from her chair. Just like he had done the first time he saw her, he now looked at Angie up and down, very slowly, and up and down again making her stomach shift uneasily.

"Come here," he motioned, wanting Angie to stand in front of him. Her mother had insisted the dress they had given her as a present was not too short, and was meant to be a mini dress for little girls, but Angie was not convinced. Tugging nervously at her new dress, she was made to twirl around.

"Look at you. Well, just look at you. Beautiful. Yes, beautiful," her father slurred as he gave her a playful slap on her bottom.

"Okay. Go on, then. Off you go. Merry Christmas."

Angie hurried away, her mother and father's laughter trailing behind her. Once inside her room, she leaned back against the door and tried to take stock of what her father had just done. She had not liked him slapping her bottom nor looking at her the way he did. His calculated glare weighed on her and she tried not to invite him into her head. Her back still leaning and pressed up very hard against the door, as if the actual process was shutting thoughts of her father out, was exhausting and, just as it did earlier, her stomach shifted. This time a wave of nausea suddenly hit her. A wave of nausea, so intense, that she very nearly did not make it to the bathroom before emptying her stomach of all the food she had so much appreciated at dinner. Hot, futile tears spilled from Angie's eyes as she whined and whimpered between each heave and spurge of nasty vomit.

CHAPTER 18

'By the pricking of my thumbs, something wicked this
way comes.'

Macbeth Act 4, Scene 1, William Shakespeare

Easter 1966

"It's called gingham, Angie. Gingham material. My
kitchen curtains are made with this and I've brought
some of the leftover pieces in for our collages. I'm glad
you like it so much. It will be interesting for me to see
how you might apply it. Good girl."

"Thank you, Mrs. Brown."

Angie thought the material very pretty and had an idea
in mind for her picture. In the Art lesson the class had
to include material as part of their design of a dream
place, where they would like to be, or a dream object
they would like to own. Angie chose a dream place as
her theme.

She was glad to be back at school and let her mind absorb positive things. She was glad to be away from the uncertainty of what each day at home could bring.

After her father slapping her bottom, she had not seen much of him for the rest of the Christmas period. She always tried her best to keep out of his way when he came home from work. It would often be quite late when he returned. Her parents would then have dinner together. Her mother's attempts at cooking usually amounted to a simple dish of beans on toast or, more often than not, she would buy a ready meal that would only need to be warmed up in the oven. Angie seldom shared in the meals, having been given permission, earlier, to grab some chocolate, or a slice of bread, and eat it quickly or take it to her room. Specific orders and instructions included the usual ones of not disturbing her mother and father and to make sure that, in the morning, she washed any pots left over from the evening meal and then cleaned round the kitchen before leaving to go to school. Angie always made sure never to neglect her duties. Even her father no longer being away did not seem to dispel her mother's vicious moods. Angie noticed that if her father did not indulge all his attention on her mother, when he was at home, then her mother would sulk and later disturb Angie's sleep with all the usual slurs:

"You think daddy being home is going to make things better for you? I've seen the way he looks at you. Well, don't be fooled. You're still an ugly, hideous and vile little girl. Ugly, hideous and vile. Yes, yes, you are."

242

Angie's dream place was a cottage far, far away, somewhere in the countryside where it was quiet and peaceful. Surrounded by trees and flowers, the cottage would be very pretty and just like the ones in all the Enid Blyton books she had read. She loved the illustrations of the quaint cottages that featured in many of the books and now took inspiration from them. She cut the blue and white gingham carefully, pasting the pieces onto her drawing and so adding just one of the finishing touches to her dream creation. A cotton candy place where she could be happy and far removed from the terror and misery that her childhood had thus far known. Angie did not know it then but her creation was soon to fill her dreams permanently, clinging on to the fantasy as she tried to escape Hell.

Bob was still able to chauffeur Angie to and from school in her father's car. For Christmas her father had acquired a new car which he used nearly all the time. It was a two seater sports car in red. It was her father's pride and joy and he would enjoy cleaning and polishing it on the drive until every inch of it was gleaming. The top of the car could even be folded back to expose the cream leather interior, however, as yet, the weather had not allowed her father to take advantage of this added feature.

Since Christmas the weather had been generally wet, cold and bleak and, as Easter approached, it showed little sign of improving. In fact, it got worse and Angie could not help thinking about what her teacher had said regarding the forces of nature and how the Elizabethans associated unnaturally bad weather with evil and the foreshadowing of something terrible about to happen.

Easter Sunday, April 10, and Angie wondered what Easter actually meant. What the class had been told was a little confusing. Christians believed that after Jesus died on a cross he was left in a cave and that, one day, when the heavy stone that was blocking the entrance was rolled away, he was gone. This was the resurrection of Jesus. She looked up the word 'resurrection' straight after she had heard it used by the teacher, and was happy to discover its meaning, yet still wondered how anyone could come back to life once they had died? After some thought she decided that, because Jesus was such a good man who helped everyone, then God brought him back for a time to do more good things and later helped him fly back up to heaven to be with him. This was as much as she knew, though, and the fact that it meant another dreaded holiday from school. She remembered the date since her teacher had made the class write it down in their homework books. They were to compose either a short essay, or a poem, about what happened to them on that day. Angie enjoyed homework and would always do it but not this time…

April, and the snow continued to fall as it had done now for days. It was very cold and blizzards fell disrupting life outside. It was Spring and meant to be sunny and mild. Not freezing.

Just like Christmas Day, her mother had arranged for caterers to prepare and serve the family dinner and, once again, Angie felt herself having to endure the company of her mother and father as they took the caterers for granted and drank too much. Still, a full meal, for once, and tasty and filling and Angie made sure to smile and thank the lady as each helping was served.

Angie could not help noticing her father's surreptitious glances in her direction as he engaged with her mother and humoured the giggles and laughter that grew louder with each glass of wine that was poured.

His glances made Angie feel uncomfortable and tense. After the meal she sat very still, not daring to move an inch. She needed to ask permission to be excused and was finally prompted by the pins and needles tingling in her hands and making them feel numb. The feeling was not pleasant and, once more, Angie recalled something else her teacher had told the class about the Elizabethans and their superstitions. She had said that, as well as very bad weather, pins and needles were also seen as a bad sign. A sign that something wrong was afoot. Something wicked and evil. Angie's mind was in turmoil and she felt like screaming. She needed to leave the table and escape to her room.

"Could I be excused, please?" she finally managed to utter.

"Pardon? What was that? You wish to be excused? Well, not before you come here and give your daddy a big hug."

Angie looked at her father's twitching smile as his bleary eyes held her gaze.

"Well? Come here, then."

Angie stood up and reluctantly made her way into the embrace her father was already offering as he rose from his seat. She could smell the alcohol, he had been drinking during the meal, and the cigarettes he had been smoking, as he held her in a tight squeeze and nuzzled his face into her hair. The hug lingered and she could not free herself. His stubbled chin grazed her cheek and his right hand started to travel slowly the distance from her shoulder to her bottom. This time he did not slap her bottom but, instead, pinched it. She managed to pull away from him, her legs all weak as she turned and walked out of the room. The pins and needles in her fingers had now spread to her toes, making the quick exit she wanted to make difficult

Her father called out, "Angie? I'll be up later to tuck you in. Yes, tonight I'll come and tuck you in. Good girl."

An unsettling fear started to build within her as she now rushed up the stairs to her room. What did her father mean? She had never been tucked in before and was not sure what it involved. One thing that was for sure, however, she did not want him to come into her room at all. She did not want him anywhere near her.

As the evening progressed the terror gripped her even more. The caterers had left some time ago after they had cleared away and had washed the pots and pans and Angie knew that, just as they had done at Christmas, the kitchen would be a gleaming showpiece. She was thankful since it meant she would not have to do anything there in the morning. All she would need to do was tidy up any mess in the living room and hope her mother had not been sick or weed on the new shag pile. The new pile was much longer and thicker and more difficult to clean. Her father never concerned himself about the messes his wife left. He expected Angie to deal with it. Angie had found this out not long after he had come home to stay. She had even caught him spying on her, once or twice, as she knelt down to do what was required, and had detected a smirk on his face; a little rise in the corner of his mouth that made her feel unsettled and discomfited.

Looking out of her bedroom window she had watched the ladies leaving earlier and wished that they could have stayed. She did not want to be left alone in the

247

house, not tonight, as she tried to shut out the raucousness of her mother's chatter and her father's deep and throaty responses, that would often filter through into every corner of every room in the house whenever they enjoyed too many drinks together.

Spring, and the flowers outside should have been coming into bud, rising from the earth and promising a rainbow garland of lovely colours in the garden. Instead, the scene outside was more like winter; its cold, freezing teeth biting and disturbing the natural order of life. As the snow continued to fall Angie shut the curtains, no longer wanting to witness the suffocation of new growth yearning to escape the blanket of snow that now had it trapped.

Her father had not yet been to tuck her in. Angie suspected that he had probably had too much to drink and had forgotten or had fallen asleep on the settee. She was glad and was able to relax a little. Her eyelids started to droop and she snuggled under her bed covers. She was happy to surrender herself to sleep, driving away all that had occurred at dinner and free now to chase her dreams. The door to her cotton candy cottage was wide open and Angie went inside.

An overpowering smell of whiskey and cigarettes later roused Angie from her sleep and her dreams. The smell arrived at the side of her bed before he did. Her father.

He had not forgotten, after all. Still somewhat drowsy Angie had sense enough to know that something was not right about this. He had come to tuck her in and, even though she did not quite know what this meant, she knew straight away that she did not want him there.

She squeezed her eyes shut trying to find her cotton candy cottage once more. She wanted to run inside and close the door. Maybe he would then go away but the cottage had gone. All that was left was a darkness so frightening she felt she could not breathe.

Even though she was silent and still, her father put his hand over her mouth as he climbed into her bed.

"Shh," he said, "shh, my darling. Daddy's here to tuck you in but first we need to do something together."

"What did he mean?" Angie's fear intensified as the question battled in her brain searching desperately for an answer.

"Mummy says you always do as you are told and you are very quick to learn. So, it's time for me to teach you things that good girls always let their daddies do. They never tell anyone, though. Never. That's the way it is, you see. If daughters tell then no-one will ever want to come near them and they won't be allowed to go to school ever again. No school will accept them since girls that tell are seen as disrespectful and very bad for telling and so not a good influence on others. Do you understand, my darling? Do you?"

With his hand still over her mouth, Angie could only nod. So much for her ten-year-old brain to fully comprehend but one thing she did latch onto was the threat of not being able to go to school. Not going to school meant no escape. Not going to school meant no more learning, no more books, all of which she could not envisage. A life she did not want.

"Well, do you understand, my darling? Do you?" he whispered in her ear as he took his hand away from her mouth.

"Yes, Daddy," Angie muttered. "Yes, Daddy, I do."

"Good girl. My good little girl."

With her eyes still shut tight Angie felt her father's hands slowly exploring every part of her body until finally putting his fingers in a very private place. Her wee wee place and she immediately tried to cross her legs so that he would not touch her there again. Her father was strong, stronger than she was and he continued to spread her legs wide apart. He made her touch something fleshy and hard. He guided her hand up and down, up and down the hard bone of flesh and then moved his body on top of her and started to force the stiffness inside her wee wee place. Her hand no longer holding the stiff bone of fleshiness, her father started to force the hardness into her pee pee place. He pushed and pushed and Angie screamed out. The pain she felt at each push was excruciating. She could not bear it. Like the blanket of snow outside suffocating the new growth of Spring yearning to escape, Angie was trapped. With eyes still tight shut she desperately tried to find her sweet cotton candy cottage, surrounded by peace and quiet and beautiful flowers and the blue and white pretty gingham curtains hanging at the windows. She could hear herself trying to catch her breath in the empty, pain-filled darkness as she desperately searched and searched, but to no avail, until her father's voice cut into the moment and he was done.

"There you go. That wasn't so bad was it? Daddy knows what he's doing. Now, mummy says to wash between your legs and to use the cold water tap only. She says you know what to do."

It was the first time he raped her and it was just the beginning. He watched her as she got out of bed and went to the bathroom to clean herself. She felt bruised down below and, when she went to pee, the pain made her feel dizzy and sick. The pain was so deep, so fierce that she thought she was going to die. She wiped away blood and cried. The blood frightened her and she wanted to scream again out loud, very loud, as the tears coursed down her cheeks and would not stop. With the soap and flannel, and cold water running freely from the tap, she washed and washed and washed away the blood and the stickiness between her legs. It was only when she heard her mother's voice coming from her parents' bedroom that she finally stopped.

"Switch that bloody tap off and get back to bed! You should be clean by now!"

Angie did as she was told. Her father was still there in her room.

"About time, too," he said, "now, get into bed and I'll tuck you in and say night, night."

Warily, Angie got back into bed. Her father tucked the sheet and blankets tight under the mattress before bending over and planting a kiss on her forehead.

"Goodnight darling. Daddy's good, little girl. Sweet dreams. Yes, sweet dreams my darling."

CHAPTER 19

'In order to rise from its own ashes, a Phoenix first
must burn.'

Octavia Butler, 1947-2006

Rebirth

Angie was too afraid to surrender herself to sleep again
that night in case her father returned. She tried   to
think about her cotton candy cottage once more but it
was no longer there and instead, when sleep finally
came, all that she could find was a small, grey, empty
room with a very frightened little girl curled up in the
corner. A very, very quiet little girl hiding away from
footsteps she could hear approaching her space. She
kept very still and very quiet hoping he would not find
her; hoping he would leave her alone and go away.

He never did leave her alone and, although sporadic at first, her father's abuse became more frequent and escalated as Angie got older. Over the years she developed valuable coping mechanisms that enabled her to disengage with the abuse when it occurred.

Christmas Day, 1968, Angie, now fourteen years old, knew exactly what to expect from her father. A Christmas present he never failed to deliver. He always made sure to tuck her in at Christmas since it was a special day; a day for rejoicing and celebration. Her coping strategies, all her mind distractions, were ready to be called into play as she waited for the inevitable to happen. That night, however, her father's abuse was raised to another level, a level so extreme, so shocking, Angie's mental control was cruelly denied.

Under the cover and darkness of her blanket, her father stood close enough for Angie to breathe in his all too familiar scent. This time, though, another scent hit her first. The sickly, sweet heady scent of her mother's perfume. On occasion her mother would watch as her husband took pleasure from what he did to Angie and then she would walk away or, sometimes, stand at the bathroom door and issue her instructions.

"Wash between your legs. Wash between your legs. Cold water! Cold water!"

Repeat. Repeat. Repeat. By now Angie knew exactly what to do and felt like screaming out at her mother but she never did. She remained submissive and compliant and never said a word or ever spoke out of turn.

"Angie? Angie? My sweet, darling little girl. Well, maybe not so little anymore, No, you are growing into something quite exquisite. Beautiful and so soft, so very soft to touch. Tonight, I have a very special treat in store for you. A very special treat indeed."

Over the years Angie had become accustomed to the usual foreplay and things that he wanted her to say to him which, although she hated saying them, she soon realised that they made the whole nasty, invasive business over with a lot quicker. Tonight was different. No foreplay as he flung the blankets back and told her to take off her knickers. Angie did as she was told, her eyes tight shut as she now started to think of which game she should play in her head by way of distraction. Before she had time to think, however, she felt her father's hands flinging her over onto her stomach, his breathing much louder and quicker and more urgent than usual. Something was wrong. She had never been made to turn over onto her stomach before. Something was not right, not right at all as he lay on top of her and she could feel his hardness rubbing over her bottom. His breathing grew heavier and heavier with each movement. Angie's fear set her heart racing as he knelt up, straddling across her bottom, and then unimaginable pain. He started to force his hardness into her bottom, forcing it and tearing and tearing the tightness with each push of extreme agony that it took her breath away. Eyes wide open now in shock and agonising pain, she stared at her mother pleading for it to stop.

She screamed out between each tortuous push, "Mummy! Mummy! Please. Please make him stop! Please!"

Her mother just looked blank, totally unmoved, totally impervious, staring and watching as her daughter's screams fell on deaf ears. Screams of wild panic, desperate and terrified and when, at last, her father had done and her mother just walked away, Angie knew something for certain. She knew now just how much she hated them. No more sense of guilt at the very thought of hating her mother and father, a feeling she had battled with for as far back as she could remember. Pain and cruelty had a limit and they had crossed it now too many times. A raging hatred filled her soul, it burned in her heart and, as she lay there on her stomach and alone, she vowed she would never let them hurt her again. Never again.

Struggling to walk to the bathroom, some time later, she could hear the snores of deep sleep coming from her parents' bedroom and the hate within her deepened. Wiping the blood away from her bottom and trying so hard to manage the stinging, burning pain that each touch rendered, Angie no longer cared about what was expected of her. She turned on the hot water tap and let it flow and run until her flannel was soaked and its heated wetness brought a measure of relief with each gentle application. A luxury denied her, except bath times which her mother still monitored and directed despite Angie's years, the hot water was now all hers to control.

The rest of the Christmas holiday, for the most part, Angie spent in her room lost in sleep; a sleep which took her away from the hurt and bruising pain she could still feel burning her bottom. A few times her mother had opened the door and thrown a bar of chocolate on the bed, telling her daughter it was time she stirred, time to stop being so soft and time she stopped feeling sorry for herself. Her mother's voice made Angie's flesh crawl as she allowed herself to own, in its entirety, the all consuming hate she felt. Hatred had armed Angie and she made sure that she had what was needed to stop her father's hurt, his evil, once and for all. She had what was needed to end her mother's cruelty, her mother's cold heart. Yes, the top drawer in the kitchen had given her options and, in the secret dead of night, not long after her father's ultimate violation, she had made her way downstairs and chosen well. Driven by loathing and the abject fear that had hounded her for so long, Angie was ready and bided her time. Her hate was further fuelled from knowing that, in a few days, the new school term was due to begin. A new year, a new year of learning and development and one which was to be denied her. One never to be fulfilled since Angie knew then that she would not be going to school ever again.

She had been expecting her father to come to her room for a few days now and, when he inevitably did, her resolve had not waned. The new year had brought with it a new Angie. No longer submissive and quiet and obedient, the fighter within her was released. He removed her knickers and knelt over her, his erection fully exposed and ready.

"Angie. My darling little girl. Now, turn over onto your tummy just like last time. Yes, like last time," he whispered.

Driven, driven, by years of pain and torment and fear, as she started to turn over, she quickly brought out the knife hidden under her pillow and, like a carefully choreographed move, she clutched it in her hand and plunged it deep into his side. A satisfying squish as the tip sank deep enough to make him gasp. She twisted and twisted the blade in her hand, her mind now empty but her move still carefully choreographed like a slow dance twisting, twisting and sinking the blade deeper and deeper; skin tearing to shreds as the knife twisted and rotated once more. As if in slow motion, mouth painfully agape, he held himself upright until she twisted and squelched the knife out. He fell forwards but not before she had rolled out of his way. She had been trapped beneath his bulk too many times before. This time, she held herself over him. With an inner strength she never knew she had, she turned him over and torn, torn and fractured from years of abuse, she stabbed and stabbed and stabbed, not knowing how many times, until she stopped; his life's source gushing out in all directions. It was all surreal. Very little noise and her mother downstairs, totally oblivious to the blood now spreading on the sheets, like a flower bursting into bloom, its red petals vibrant and intense, her mother still watching the television and waiting for her husband to join her once he had tucked his little girl in.

Lost now in a vast wilderness of negative emotions, naked and bloody, the knife still in her hand, Angie made her way downstairs to the front room.

Lounging on the settee, a glass of the clear liquid in her hand; the clear liquid she loved more than anything else in her life, except herself, her mother's glazed eyes, half shut, did not register at first Angie's presence. Angie stared at this woman whose cold heart could never bring itself to love but instead flaunted an indifference that had drained Angie's life for so long; an indifference, an emptiness that cared not if her daughter suffered; an emptiness that had actively caused so much suffering, too. Clinging on to the poison now fuelling her brain, and before her mother could say a word, Angie lunged forward and plunged the blade deep into her mother's belly. She twisted and turned and twisted and twisted, turned and turned the blade before bringing it out. Her mother groaned and gurgled as she bled and Angie wanted her quiet and gone. The fear and the dread that had been a constant in her life, drowning her soul, drowning her spirit Angie wanted it gone and she stabbed over and over again.

"Hideous! Vile! Ugly!"

Stab. Stab. Stab.

"Ugly! Ugly!"

Stab. Stab.

Frenzied and wild, her rage firing itself further, she grabbed the vodka bottle from the side table, its top already removed just waiting to be poured. She poured the clear liquid onto her mother's lap. Angie watched as its wetness pooled with the blood now drenching the fine pastel coloured fabric of her mother's dress and flowing, like a red river, onto the settee's creamy leather upholstery.

"Wash between your legs. Cold water. Cold water. Cold water. You dirty, dirty, vile, ugly little girl!"

She looked up at her mother's glassy, staring eyes.

"Stop it! Stop it! Stop watching! Stop watching!" she screamed and, finally, smashing the empty bottle still in her hands, she stabbed the glassy orbs that had watched her daughter's misery and pain for years. Never again. No, never again. A blanket of red, beautiful bright red, like her teacher's lipstick, calmed Angie's rage. It was all that was left of her mother and Angie was done.

Stepping back now, Angie suddenly felt sick and dizzy and a throbbing pain in her head rooted itself so deep she shut her eyes tight, squeezing them and willing the pain to go away. The throbbing whirled itself round and round like a mist at the edges of her mind, eventually draining her into sweet oblivion as she collapsed in a heap on the thick pile of the cream carpet.

The gas fire still burning and radiating a much needed warmth and the hissing, crackling, sound of the television's fuzzy screen indicating an end to the evening's transmission, were the first things Angie registered when she came round some time later. Still naked, the blood congealed and smelly covering her skin like a weird and confusing abstract design, Angie lay still and did not move. The stench of her mother was nasty and strong, a familiar smell reminding Angie of her first day at school when she had soiled her knickers.

She needed time now to shed the deep oblivion of her fainting sleep and to process her thoughts. She needed time to find solutions to the nightmare that was now fixed and real in the bloody messes she had left behind. She knew she would have to get away. She would have to get herself clean and ready for a journey into the unknown, a journey that somehow did not frighten her. She had been frightened too many times before and had now found the strength to rid herself of the unfailing torment that had plagued her life. The chains that had tied her to so much unspoken pain, terrible pain, were now broken and she felt empowered.

The warmth from the gas fire eased her stiff limbs as she sat up slowly. Hugging her knees, and rocking backwards and forwards, slowly, backwards and forwards, over and over, just as she had done many times before and ever since her father's first abuse of power, she stared at the flickering flames that seemed to aid and calm the pattern of her thoughts. She stole a quick glance at the clock on the wall and then resumed her concentrated gaze. It was just gone four in the morning. There was no need to rush. No one would be coming. For some reason Judita only ever came now once a week on Tuesdays and a new lady, Brenda, came on Thursdays to do the cleaning and whatever else she was instructed to do. Angie did not really know Brenda. She never acknowledged Angie when she saw her and was always grim faced. Angie was only sorry that it would be Judita who next came to the house once she had gone.

Standing up, she switched off the fire and the now annoying crackling, fuzzy, fluttering of transmission ended on the television. Without once looking at the bloodied, grisly heap of her mother, Angie left the room and made her way upstairs to the bathroom. Instant hot water and the forbidden shower beckoned.

The shower was a luxury never before afforded to her and now there was no one there and nothing to stop this privilege. As the steaming cascade of water showered over her body, cleansing away all evidence of her foulness, of the horrid act she had committed, Angie's thoughts halted suddenly. No! They were the ones to blame for what she had done and she made herself accept this now. They were vile. They were foul. They were rotten, rotten to the core and now their vileness, their 'bloody' vileness was being washed away. Angie watched its red drizzle turn to pink, staining the bath and the white surround tiles as she stood there embracing the cleansing power of the hot water on her mind as well as her body.

Eventually, turning off the shower, she carefully stepped out of the bath leaving the stained mess behind. There was no need for her to clean it. There was no need for her to clean anywhere in this horrid mausoleum ever again.

Her mind now a lot more alert, Angie knew she still had things to do. She needed clean underwear and some clothes. They were in her room. She did not look at what was left of her father lying on the bed as she quickly retrieved what was needed. She would need money and went to see what she could find in their bedroom. Her mother's purse was empty of notes but there was some change. Her father's wallet, on the bedside cabinet, also yielded little but there were some notes that would help her to get as far away from this hell as possible. She felt no guilt or shame in stealing from them. Not now. Now, she was on her own and she was glad.

She knew she should not draw attention to herself, and so, packing a suitcase and taking it with her, was not a good idea. So many thoughts were invading and spinning around in her head that she felt she needed to lie down and sleep away the panic that was threatening to attack. The clock on her father's bedside cabinet registered 6:30 am. It was still early. There was time to rest, time to build the strength and reserve much needed to embark on the next journey in her life.

She opened the door to one of the spare bedrooms, a door rarely opened except for when Judita, or now Brenda, gave it its weekly once over. Another beautiful room, for show only, and now Angie invited herself to lie down and let sleep steady her concerns and put to rest the horror she had lived, the whole sorry story of her life so far.

She opened the cupboard door and brought out the box that was hiding away in its deepest, darkest recess. She opened the box and, one by one, she packed away every single, sordid, nasty, frightening memory of the place she was leaving behind. Hell, and its demons. She closed the lid. She pushed the box back into the cupboard; way, way back once again into its deepest, darkest recesses and slammed the door shut…

Sleep calmed her whirling fears and panic and, when Angie finally woke, she knew she must have been lost in her exhaustion for hours and was thankful. Sleep had shown her a cupboard door and a box now hiding away in there. Her mental cupboard and one she had no need to open ever again.

She was ready to leave. Glancing at the bedside clock she was surprised to see it was now getting quite late. It was just after three. She wanted to leave before it started to get dark. She had decided to get the bus into the main depot in town and then another bus to somewhere, anywhere as far away as possible. She had not thought beyond that and for now she did not want to. First things first.

She got dressed quickly and hurried downstairs to the kitchen, at the same time double checking that she had put the money she would need, safely inside her jeans' pocket.

It was Friday and the cupboards were almost bare. She had some cereal and milk and a glass of water. She looked for chocolate to take with her but there was none to be had. No doubt her mother would have been going to get some today to replenish the cupboard where it was usually housed. Shopping for easy luxuries, like biscuits and chocolates, her mother could manage herself when she went to buy the beloved bottles of clear liquid that she could not live without. All the other groceries, of course, were left to Judita. Yes, Judita. Angie would miss her. She would miss Bob, too. Even though he had stopped taking her to school, once she had started at the local grammar and old enough to get the bus, he had always given her a thumbs up and a smile whenever he saw her looking through the window.

She knew it would be cold outside and suddenly realised her duffle coat was hanging up in her wardrobe. She could not bring herself to go back there and, instead, took her mother's coat that she knew would be hanging up in the downstairs' closet. The coat was heavy and too big for her but it was warm and would stave off the biting harshness of any extreme weather. The pockets were deep. She removed the money from her jeans and put it safe inside one of the pockets before opening the front door. Straightaway, the cold and wind hit her. She wrapped the thick, heavy coat, with its fur collar, and her mother's stale perfume trapped amongst its itchy fibres, tightly round her slight frame, slammed the door shut and, without looking back, braved whatever lay ahead…

The silence that ensued when she had finished telling me her story was not awkward at all. We had been through so many moments of reflection that I knew it was only a matter of time before she would look at me and speak once more. A number of times she would remain lost in her thoughts for the rest of the session and I knew to just wait patiently and be there for her. As it was, this time, it did not take her long to say something.

"Well, that's it. You know the rest. Yes, you know the rest."

She looked at me as I nodded and offered a reassuring smile.

"Yes, Angie, I know the rest."

With a pained look of concern on her face she halted a little before speaking again.

"Rosie? Rosie? Do you think I'm bad? Do you think I'm vile? Do you?"

I knew that my answer mattered. My answer mattered so much to her.

"No, Angie, I don't think you are bad or vile. What I do know is that you have suffered alone for so long that something inside you snapped. It made you want to stop what was happening in a way that was, in that moment, the only thing you thought to do to end everything."

"Rosie? I need to tell you something else."

"Okay?"

"I don't regret what I did, you know. I don't regret it at all. The only things I regret are losing Jimmy and for any trouble I might have brought Alice."

I was able to tell her, at this point, that Alice was fine. After being questioned by the police they had to let her go. No had come forward to say anything about her or the type of house she kept. People only had good things to say about her and so, what they knew about Alice taking in a lodger, to look after her and do the cleaning, was confirmed. Jimmy used to run errands for Alice and knew that she needed a housekeeper and so, after first meeting Angie at the bus station, he took her to the house. As far as the police were concerned Jimmy was a waif and stray that Alice had taken pity on and he would often help her out when needed and vice versa.

I was also able to tell her that, after all that had happened, Alice and her neighbour, Aggie, had decided to move away and go live with Aggie's brother in a lovely little village just outside the town. Aggie's brother had been recently widowed and needed some help to run his fruit and vegetable shop in the village. Alice was happy to help out in the shop a few days a week and had even started to lose weight!

All this information I had gleaned from a letter I had written to Alice once I had found out where she had moved to. I somehow knew how much it would matter to Angie to know how things had turned out for Alice. One could say Alice's story indeed had a 'happy ever after'.

Angie smiled but the pained look of concern, that I had seen so many times before, surfaced once more.

"Does she think badly of me? Do you think she will ever forgive me?"

It was enough for me to tell Angie that Alice had asked after her and sent her love.

Angie smiled again.

This was to be our last session together now that Angie had finished her story. We both knew that it would be and she now seemed resigned to await the outcome of what she had done.

"Do you know, Rosie, it's not so bad here. I feel safe. There's no one here that can hurt me. They even have a library. Did you know?"

I nodded.

"Yes, a library and they have even said that I can help out there. So, I have books to read. "The Giving Tree", which you bought me, is on the shelf in my room and I read it nearly every day. Each time I look at it I remember my beautiful teacher with her red lipstick and now I also think of you."

I needed to go. We said our goodbyes, my professionalism struggling to keep in check as I wanted to hug her, and tell her that all would be well and come right one day, but I did not.

Outside, after a very unsettled start to the weather so far in May, the rain clouds had shifted and the sun had started to shine. At last I could bring out the new designer sunglasses that I had saved up for, and strike a pose. They were in my handbag today and I so much wanted to wear them now as I made my exit. A pair of beautifully framed shades can hide a multitude of feelings that the eyes may often betray. I did not, however. I composed myself and said a final goodbye before turning round.

269

"Oh, by the way, Rosie, just one last thing. I started my period today."

Back still turned, I nodded my head and left the room. Once outside on the long, stark, seemingly endless expanse of corridor, I quickly brought out my designer shades and struck a much needed pose as the tears threatened to overwhelm me.

EPILOGUE

Angie Ross. Complex? Undoubtedly so. A life compounded by so much hurt and misery. An amalgamation of constant fear, constant dread and abuse, emotional and physical, one can only conclude that it is not surprising everything about this young girl was complex. Influenced? Undoubtedly. So many variables, so many staggering episodes and stimuli made this young girl break and, in the end, kill.

People tend to view killers as absolutely evil beings or ones so damaged they cannot possibly live among society ever again. Indeed, there are some. However, there are those that are, themselves, untreated, traumatised children who never stand a chance. Trauma is fundamental but it is difficult for society to see that part of it. Society sees the result of trauma rather than its origins.

Angie's trauma manifested itself in a way that the judge could only determine one sentence. Angie Ross was eventually found guilty of manslaughter, on the grounds of diminished responsibility, and sentenced to an indefinite term, in a young offender's institution and

271

then an open prison, until such time she would no longer be deemed a threat to society.

I know that, in time, Angie Ross will grow strong and, from her destructive childhood, build a healthier, unbroken view of herself. Something tells me that one day she will be free to live her cotton candy dream.

'Dreams are cherished gifts of the mind, just waiting to be opened. Never lose sight of them.'

L. M. Kimblin

NOTE FROM THE AUTHOR

The ending of my story, and what Angie Ross/Jenny Smith was driven to do, is not easy for my reader but it is, I feel, an important reminder that some stories are simply tragic and a tragedy, such as this, should be dogged and unflinching in its telling.

2020 lockdown, and I should have been marking GCSE English Language papers in my role as an examiner. However, COVID-19 put paid to this and the education norm for children and young students across the world was unprecedentedly halted.

After 33 years teaching English in the same marvellous school, I took early retirement in 2012. Teaching for me was an invaluable experience where each day brought with it so many challenges yet so many joys and I loved it. Yes, it was tiring. Yes, it was frustrating. Yes, it was difficult at times yet the positives far outweighed the negatives. Teaching is never just a one way process. For me, the delight was that I learned so much from my students and valued very much their opinions, their thoughts, their stories, their moans and groans, their laughter and their tears. To this day I have stayed in touch with a number of them and look forward to coffee catch-ups when we can.

Sadly, my husband and I found out very early on in our marriage that it would be a chance in a million if I were ever to conceive. I never did conceive and we came to accept it. Being surrounded, day in and day out, by young individuals, teaching helped me so much with my acceptance and the fact that my husband and I could not have children of our own. My husband has always been my mainstay and we always said that had we been able to have a boy we would have called him George. Instead, we had cats! After 42 years of marriage we now have George IV and he's gorgeous!

Writing this story made me consider how very different life could have been for my protagonist had she been born into a loving and caring family. All her potential, so cruelly denied and all the suffering so cruelly inflicted by those that should have been her protectors.

My own mother and father worked hard to give my beautiful older sister, Rosanna, and me a good education and we thrived in their love. My home was a mix of languages and cultures with a wonderful Ukrainian father and a quirky, equally wonderful Italian mother. Diverse cultures and languages and, the irony of it all, I ended up teaching English! Sadly, we lost Rosanna in 2009 after her brief battle with cancer. A terrible time. Along with my parents she too gave me everything and more and now they surround me with their love from Heaven above.

If I were to be a cameo in my story I would be the grammar school girl in the library that smiles at Jenny. After school my friends and I would sometimes go to the library in town. We would sit upstairs in the private study areas trying hard to revise or do homework but, more often than not, surreptitiously chatting and giggling. A few times my mother would meet me outside, after having been in town, and together we would walk home, linking arms.

Growing up can be a tumultuous time. Children need the support of parents who must give them room to develop and help them confront difficult issues. Unfortunately, for a number of children this is not the case. Lockdown 2020 news documented a concerning rise in the reported cases of abuse and how, for many children and young people, there was no escape from the home. I found the reports quite harrowing and then I recalled a book that I had come across a few years ago in one of the local charity shops. I needed something to read and was in a bit of a hurry. I was drawn by the title of a hard backed tome which stood out from the rest: 'Dark Heart'. Without reading any of the blurb, I paid a customary two pounds and left. However, once I started reading the book I felt that paying just two pounds was cheating the author. The book turned out to be an eye-opener, an outstanding piece of journalism detailing the ' threads of Britain's twisted social fabric... following the trail of the street children through corruption and violence… ' and so much more. Investigative journalist, Nick Davies, takes us with him

275

on his journey and reveals, 'The Shocking Truth about Hidden Britain'. I found his revelations uncomfortable. Indeed, I took the idea of an eleven-year-old 'rent boy' from one of the characters Nick Davies actually met. I mention a 'card school' in my story which is something else I learned about from Nick Davies' disclosures.

Lockdown 2020 saw me putting pen to paper and deciding to at last write the novel so many of us say we would like to do but never actually find time. No excuses now! I started to conduct some research of my own on children in circumstances that made me so grateful for the blessed upbringing that I had. However, my research also led me into a subject that is so dark and disturbing but does exist and I was drawn. I needed to understand why children and young people kill a parent or both. Parricide.

There are three types of individuals who commit parricide. One is the severely abused child who is pushed to his/her limits. Another is the severely mentally ill child and the third is the dangerously antisocial child.

The severely abused child is the most frequent type of offender and this is where my protagonist finds herself. These individuals kill because they can no longer tolerate conditions at home. They have been abused by one or both parents and have often suffered physical, sexual, emotional and verbal abuse. Not criminally sophisticated at all. For them, an act of desperation - the only way out of a situation they can no longer endure.

Isolated, not merely by a burden of abuse but by a burden of shame.

The true killer is child maltreatment. The true killer is abuse.

About the Author

L. M. Kimblin was born in Bolton, Lancashire, in the 1950's. She grew up in a home of diverse cultures, Ukrainian and Italian, both of which blessed and shaped her life in all the right directions. She studied English and Art at Sedgley Park Teacher Training College in Prestwich, Manchester, and went on to teach English, for the next 33 years in the same school, until taking early retirement in 2012. Enjoying lots of quality retirement time, lockdown 2020 put paid to all her usual activities and pursuits and provided an opportunity to turn her hand to writing her debut novel, 'Cotton Candy'. She will be celebrating her 42nd wedding anniversary this year and lives with husband Keith and cat, George IVth, in the Horwich countryside near Bolton. She enjoys listening to tranquil piano music, being 'arty' and adding to her shoe collection!

Printed in Great Britain
by Amazon